CHRONICLES OF G.A.I.A.

NORBU'S SECRET

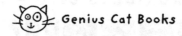 Genius Cat Books

an imprint of Kayppin Media

www.geniuscatbooks.com
Parkland, FL

ABOUT THIS BOOK
Text was set in Termina, TurnipRE and Helvetica.
Text copyright © 2024 by Dana Klisanin.
Artwork by Melisca Klisanin
Artwork Copyright is held by © Evolutionary Guidance Media R&D, Inc.
Book design by Melisca Klisanin.

All rights reserved. No part of this publication may be reproduced or distributed in any form or by any means without prior written consent from publisher.

Library of Congress Control Number: 2023938666
ISBN: 9781962447171 (hardcover)

First edition, 2024

Our books may be purchased in bulk for promotional, educational, or business use. For more information, or to schedule an event, please visit geniuscatbooks.com.

Printed and bound in China.

CHRONICLES OF G.A.I.A.
NORBU'S SECRET

Dana Klisanin

Illustrated by:
Melisca Klisanin

To Pachamama, the Achuar People, Indigenous communities, and all who tirelessly protect the delicate web of life, dreaming a new dream for our world.

—DK

If the world is to be healed through human efforts, I am convinced it will be by ordinary people, people whose love for this life is even greater than their fear.

–Joanna Macy

Prologue

"Zara, slow down!" I call, chasing the agile form of my Saluki through the forest. The fog has rolled in from the sea and mist hangs low in the canopy—a haunting, otherworldly melody wafts through the trees. Zara darts between them, following the sound, her feathered tail blending into the mist. She's white, not blue, so I know I'm dreaming.

"Woof," she howls but doesn't turn or slow. I pump my legs harder, trying to catch up, but the spongy forest floor slows me down. My sneakers are soaking wet, and my feet are heavy.

"Wait for me," I shout. My heart pounds, sweat trickles down my forehead, stinging my eyes. I blink it away, trying to catch sight of my dream-traveling hound.

The melody grows stronger, and I hear a far-off voice rising within it.

"Lexa!" the voice calls, each syllable stretched thin across the cosmos.

But it's not Zara.

"Hurry!" the voice insists.

"Norbu!" My voice cracks with recognition.

"Hurry, Lexa!" His voice fades in and out. "Don't stop!"

But I can't pick up my feet. I look down. The ground beneath me is shifting—morphing. The soil is wet and mucky. I'm running in place while the ground moves.

Can he see me? Does he know how hard I'm trying to reach him?

"Norbu! Where are you?" I shout.

A bank of heavy white fog hangs in the air, the melody changes, the notes rise and fall, the ground quakes, the trees tremble—ahead a streak of gold twists through the trees—Zara has become a jaguar!

"Over here," Norbu calls.

The jaguar races toward the sound of his voice.

I push my chest out and pump my legs harder, breaking free, running faster and faster—my lungs burn. The haunting melody intensifies, the acrid smell of smoke assaults me, up ahead, the jaguar leads.

"Almost . . . there . . ." I gasp.

"Lexa, act now!" Norbu yells, his voice desperate.

I leap forward, arms outstretched, bounding across the chasms of time and space.

Chapter One

I jolt upright, gasping for air, drenched in sweat, heart pounding.

It's the first time I've dreamed of Norbu—and it's unlike any dream I've ever had. It was like I was awake while I was asleep.

I grab my journal from the nightstand, desperate to capture the details, but as I write, they slip away. I read over the words. They feel empty. Something crucial is missing. The harder I try to remember, the faster the dream fades.

The light-catcher in my window reflects my mood. I slump down in my bed, close my eyes, and pull the heavy quilt over my shoulders. It feels good to be back home in my bed after that thin, lumpy cot-bed at Thistleton. There's a huge part of me that wants to stay here. To forget Norbu and everything he said. To pretend that he never contacted me. That somehow all the critical missions he tasked us with will take care of themselves.

An unpleasant tightness wells up inside my chest. I feel it every day. Part of me thinks it's because it's time for us to leave Ferndale, and part of me thinks it's because the more I learn the more I realize how big the climate crisis is. And I'm scared because I don't think we can tackle it.

My therapist, Aunt Marge, says it's called "eco-anxiety," and she's seeing other kids who are experiencing it, too. I clutch my locket and the little key that hangs beside it, taking deep breaths to calm down. Aunt Marge says that anxiety is a normal, natural response to the uncertainty we're facing in the world.

I glance at the stack of books she gave me and remind myself to start reading them and talk to the team—in case they're feeling it, too.

Norbu's absence hasn't helped. Sure, he said he wouldn't be able to stay in touch, but total radio silence? Or would that be total muon-silence? I try to shake off the memory of the last time I saw him in the airship, but the neon-green snake strangling his blue body comes vividly to mind.

Who or what was attacking him? He made it clear that our actions are tied to the future, but how closely are they tied to Norbu directly? Is he in danger right now?

Or is he angry? Does he wish he'd contacted someone else, another team?

It's been six weeks since we escaped from

Thistleton Academy and exposed their ties to Chronnite on social media. Since then, we've been developing Mission: G.A.I.A. to recruit others to help Norbu's organization prevent a looming mass extinction event.

Sure, it's been great sleeping in my bed, and I know Jack's enjoyed being home with his parents, but we've hung out in Ferndale long enough. Norbu said we needed to act fast to keep the mass extinction event at bay. Six weeks is nearly two months. Suddenly it feels like forever.

Maybe I dreamed about Norbu because I feel guilty for hanging out at home for so long. *Yeah, that's probably it.*

Of course, it's not all my fault. We could have left two weeks ago if Dad and the boys hadn't taken apart the van! My head pounds at the thought of it. *What were they thinking?*

Dad's love for anything mechanical and Will's curiosity about the quantum physics involved, combined with Jack's overall car craziness, turned the van into a heap of morphing metal parts that took *way* too long to reassemble.

The upside was the discovery of some cool future-tech gadgets Shamblin hid in secret compartments. It's unclear what some of them do, but now everyone has a wearable device that syncs with mine.

A realization hits.

Mom and Dad say they're supportive, but every day they come up with something else to keep us home. A feeling of urgency overcomes me. I get up and head downstairs, determined to leave today no matter what they have to say.

To my surprise, when I enter the kitchen, the countertop is lined with snack trays and my friends are already eating breakfast.

"Are these for us?" I ask.

"Yes, and a small gathering of soon-to-be friends," Mom replies, glancing at Jack, Will, and Sage.

I snatch a cucumber. "Can we take the leftovers with us?" I ask, reaching for the key to the van.

Before my fingers touch it, Dad grabs the key, holding it in one hand between us. "In a hurry?" he asks, his voice light but his face serious, making me wonder what's going on.

I laugh, playing along. "Oh, you know, just saving the future."

Dad frowns. "Do you think one more day is going to make a difference?"

"Is that a trick question?" I gulp, suddenly realizing he isn't joking, and try again to reach for the key. "Come on."

But Dad pulls it away.

"Is this about driving?" I ask. Dad has spent a good portion of the last ten days teaching us how to drive. "Remember," I remind him, "it's a self-driving vehicle. And we passed your driving test, just in case we ever need to override the A.I."

"You did, but . . ."

"But, what?" I cut in. "We need to pack and get going. Norbu is counting on us!"

Mom places a hand on my shoulder before I can say more. "Lexa," she says softly, "will you please slow down for a minute?"

"Slow down? You guys know we're leaving today."

"No, not today," Dad says firmly.

I feel like a neon green snake is strangling me. "What? You can't do this!"

"We can and we are." Dad holds up the key. "If what you've told us is true—and we have no reason to doubt it—your lives are in danger. We weren't the only ones who saw that hologram of Zara, or that airship. Chronnite will be coming after you and it's our responsibility to protect you and your friends."

My heart races. "Have you been pretending to support us?" I shout. "Just to keep us from leaving? What kind of environmental activists are you anyway? Norbu said the future is in danger. Mega-crises—the kind of stuff you guys say you care about!"

I clench my fists, struggling to calm down, but a weird mix of outrage and panic is building up inside me. Part of me expected my parents to want to protect us, but at the same time, I've watched them fight for environmental justice my whole life. Plus, the nightmare has me feeling guilty for staying home so long.

"Calm down, Lexa," Dad says gently. "We have a plan." He glances at my friends before continuing, "Isn't that right?"

"Wait, you guys know about this?" I spin around, glaring at my friends.

No one has the guts to look at me. Jack shoves spoonfuls of cereal into his mouth and stares at a Minecraft tutorial. Will sits beside him crunching on a piece of toast, his eyes glued to Anatola's journal like it has instructions for a time machine. Sage braids and unbraids her hair, peering out the window.

"What's going on?" I demand. "Since when do you guys go behind my back and make plans with my parents?"

"You tell her," Will says, looking at Jack.

Jack frowns. "I thought we were doing this together."

"Someone better tell me before I explode."

"Sit down, Lexa," Jack says.

"I'd rather stand alone than sit with traitors."

"Hey," Sage yells. "We're not traitors! We miss our parents, okay, and they're coming to visit us."

"What?" I stammer. "Why didn't anyone tell me about this? We're supposed to leave today. When are they arriving?"

"Uh," Will says, glancing at his watch. "T-minus 60."

My face feels hot. "One hour? How long have you guys known about this?" I ask, glaring at the journal reader first.

A heavy silence hangs in the air.

"Being in Ferndale around your parents and Jack's parents made us homesick," Sage confides, gesturing at Will. "When your mom suggested we invite them, we jumped at the chance."

I glance at Mom. She's biting her bottom lip, her face contorted in that familiar 'see what we were trying to tell you' expression.

I'm at a loss for words. While it's a relief that my parents weren't trying to keep us from leaving, I wasn't expecting this. Sage's voice saying 'homesick' hit me like a punch in the gut. I thought my friends loved it here—maybe even more than I did.

Sage had hung out at Russ Park and spent

hours learning about temperate rainforests—that is, when she wasn't tending her bonsai, or sketching rare orchids and ferns in Mom's greenhouse.

The boys had caught up on gaming and rewatched their favorite superhero movies. The rest of the time, they were busy dismantling the van and testing the tech they'd found—wearables, smartphones, spy gadgets, noise-makers, and emergency supplies.

I thought my friends were having a blast. How could I have been so oblivious to the way they were feeling? Maybe I spent too much time on social media... sure, I was trying to stay on top of the latest environmental news, but sometimes I got sucked into the funny reels. Okay, a lot of times.

I palm my face and turn to my friends. "I'm sorry, I should've realized you guys were missing your families. It'll be great to meet your parents. How long are they staying?"

"We've invited them to spend the weekend," Mom replies.

I smile. "Great, so we'll leave bright and early Monday morning."

"Lexa," Dad says, "there's a bit more to it than a visit. Their parents will need to give them permission to go with you."

Permission? The words hit like a double punch. *Asking for permission to protect the future is ridiculous.*

"Lexa, it's against the law for us to knowingly put your friends in danger," Dad explains.

My heart races. I turn to Sage and Will. "Do you think they'll give you permission?"

"We've been brainstorming ideas with your parents," Will says. "But it's not going to be easy." He hesitates. "My dad might not think four kids can make much of an impact. He'll probably suggest we take summer jobs in the Sustainability Department at Fidy—he's president of the department so it would be easy for him to arrange."

Sage shrugs. "Honestly, I'm not sure what my mom will say, but I sure do miss her. Did I ever tell you how she makes these cute little butterfly bandages for her patients? Or how good her lasagna is? Or that she has a green thumb just like me?"

My legs feel unsteady. I sink into a nearby chair. I know I should care about my friends' feelings, but all I can think about is how I might be losing my team. What if their parents won't allow them to come with me and Jack?

A crazy thought jumps into my head. I turn to face Jack. "Your parents gave you permission, right?"

"Uh," he mumbles, "not yet. They want to meet the other parents, and sort of make a mutual decision."

"Wait a minute," I groan. "Is some kind of democratic vote going to happen?" I wrap my arms around my stomach, feeling sick with the thought that Mission: G.A.I.A. might end before it has the chance to begin.

I feel a hand touch my shoulder and look up to see Mom smiling down at me, reassuringly. "It's going to be alright, Lexa," she says softly. "You just need to come up with an argument they can't refuse. Show them why what you're doing is important. Help them understand that you're not just gallivanting around on a wild goose chase. You can do it. I believe in you."

I cringe, feeling a flush of embarrassment at Mom's choice of words. Why does she always have to say things like that? Why was I born to anachronists? It's so frustrating.

Chapter Two

Climbing the stairs to my bedroom, I think about how weird it is to be back home with restrictions like this. One day I'm talking to a holographic blue boy from the future, plotting an escape from Thistleton, surviving a snowstorm, and communicating with my dead dog, and the next, I'm being told what I can and cannot do. There's something so twisted about it. How ironic would it be to escape Thistleton only to end up being told no by our parents?

I'm feeling pessimistic when I take a seat on the floor beside my friends. "We don't have much time to prepare an argument. You guys left me out of this, so maybe you can come up with a way to convince them."

"Hey," Sage says. "We didn't tell you because we figured you'd act like this."

"Sorry," I groan. "It's just that coming up with an argument that will convince your parents to let you set out in a van that morphs into an airship to tackle a series of critical missions to save the future seems sort of impossible." The words spew out of my mouth. "Plus, I feel stupid that I thought my parents were on board with our plans."

Will clears his throat. "Look, we haven't given up, so neither should you. We've already agreed not to tell them about Chronnite or any of the futuristic stuff. Zara, Norbu and Pasha, the airship, B.E.L.A., the quantum tech . . . all of it can stay on the down low unless we're directly questioned about it."

"You all sure left me out of a lot of conversations," I pout.

Jack shrugs. "Lexa, it was one conversation, and that stuff was sort of like the elephant in the room."

I should be glad my friends have given some thought to all this, but I'm still stinging from being left out. "Anything else I need to know?"

"No," Jack replies. "We just need to convince our parents that we have run some calculations and deduced that there are a specific series of critical missions that have the potential to change the course of the future . . . and we're the ones who can accomplish them."

"Uhm," Will says. "We also need to convince them we don't need to go to school because we're developing Mission: G.A.I.A. and essentially homeschooling ourselves through online resources and in-person, community-building activities."

Sage laughs nervously. "The worst part will be telling them about the self-driving van."

There's a collective sigh. We're up against a wall and need to come up with a convincing argument, and fast. But where do we even begin?

"Let's do a ten-minute meditation to clear our minds," Sage suggests.

I'm not eager to meditate but talking in circles is making me nervous. "Sure, let's do it."

Sage smiles. "Great, find a comfortable position and relax. Remember, all you need to do is follow your breath, all the way in and all the way out. When thoughts come, don't follow them, just let them go and return to your breath."

She sets the timer and I start following my breath. I can't complete two breathing cycles without getting lost in my thoughts. *What if their parents say no? Will my parents let me go alone? Do I even want to go alone? What happens to the future if I do nothing? Is it even my responsibility?*

Then, the thoughts I've been suppressing since we arrived in Ferndale burst through. *Why isn't Zara showing up when I summon her? Did I break the wearable? Where is Norbu? Why doesn't he come to help us get out of Ferndale?*

I hear a soft chime. The meditation session is ending, and I've done nothing but chase thoughts. In a few seconds, everyone opens their eyes.

"Our challenge," Sage says, like she's stumbled onto a solution, "is sort of like making the wind visible."

I like the way Sage thinks, but this is too cryptic. "Tell us more."

She shrugs nonchalantly. "We're a powerful force but no one can see us. They just see kids. The wind is invisible like we are to them. The movement of the leaves through the trees makes the wind visible, and the wind blows the seeds around. We need to think like a tree to make ourselves visible."

"That's cool," Will says.

Sage smiles.

"But how do we apply it?" Jack says what I'm thinking.

"We need to make them see us. Show them that even though we're kids, we have the power to change things," Will explains.

"Exactly." Sage beams.

Jack absentmindedly shuffles a deck of cards. "What if we talk about chaos theory? You know, just like Norbu explained it to us: how the flapping of a butterfly's wings can cause a hurricane."

Will nods. "Yeah, we may be young, but we have the potential to change the course of the future. Heck, we are the future. We should have a say in it."

I like the direction this is going. "We can share some stories about kids who made a difference," I say, crossing the room to search my bookshelves. "I've got a ton of books about kids like that." I pass a few around. "Okay, this is the best argument we've got, so let's gather our evidence, prepare our statements, and get ready to convince our parents that we're not just kids playing around."

The room buzzes with energy as we dive into our research.

We're practicing our speeches when the doorbell rings. Sage leaps up and rushes from the room. Will bounds down the stairs behind her. Jack heads out next and I trudge down last. My eyes fall on an ornately framed photograph of Great Aunt Beatrice.

I can't help but wonder what she would have done if she were alive. She would be outraged to know the nonprofit she founded has business dealings with Chronnite. I'm sure she would have fired Mr. Milnex immediately. But Dad doesn't have that kind of authority.

My thoughts are interrupted by the sounds of reunion in the foyer below.

"Mom, Dad!" Will exclaims, throwing his arms around his parents. "I've missed you guys!"

"Oh my!" Mrs. Scott gasps. "Just look how tall you've grown!"

"Mom!" Sage shouts.

"Sweetheart," Ms. Paterson says, pulling Sage into a tight hug. "I'm so glad you're okay."

After a few moments of tearful embraces and relieved laughter, Mom invites everyone into the parlor. I wonder if they know that parlor is an old-fashioned word for living room. And if they already know my parents are . . . uhm . . . retro-challenged? There are worse things than being from a family of anachronists, but I'm always on edge when we're meeting people for the first time.

A soft murmur of conversation and the occasional clink of glasses fill the room as my friends catch up with their parents.

"Thank you all for agreeing to come out here," Dad says. "We know it's a long way to travel, but the kids have been through quite an ordeal. We're proud of Lexa and I know you are equally proud of your children." He looks at me and smiles. "Lexa, would you like to say a few words?"

Dad's smile is encouraging, but I'm nervous.

"Uhm," I say, "I know it must have been shocking for you to learn about, uhm, what's going on at Thistleton. It's worse than, uhm, you might even know, so we'd like to share something important with you."

Will must feel my nerves because he comes to my rescue. "Thistleton did away with their green school program and pulled the plug on promoting creativity in favor of supporting the status quo. They were bought out by Chronnite, a corporation that's involved in stuff like turning rainforests into pasture land and expanding oil production in the Arctic. We've been studying climate science and believe we must embark on a specific series of missions to help save our planet."

"Climate science?" Mr. Scott beams. "Well, well! I never thought I'd see the day you'd be interested in anything beyond the physics of time travel!"

Mr. Scott is pleased. It feels like we're off to a good start.

Jack's up next. "Our research shows that human actions impact the climate. If we continue on our current path, the consequences will be disastrous—rising sea levels, extreme weather events, loss of biodiversity..."

Sage stands. "Many people think that kids like us can't make a difference, but we want to show you that we can. We've been learning about chaos theory, and how even small actions can have a huge impact on the future."

"Like the flapping of a butterfly's wings," I add. "It may seem insignificant, but it has the potential to set off a storm in another part of the world. We believe that together our actions have the potential to change the future."

The room falls silent for a moment as the grownups absorb our impassioned words.

"Lexa," Mrs. Scott asks, "how do you plan to make a difference? What is it you all want to do?"

"We've devised a series of missions," I reply confidently.

"Each mission targets a specific aspect of climate change. We've already begun researching renewable energy sources, ways to protect endangered species, and methods of reducing waste and pollution. And we're developing a site called Mission: G.A.I.A., based around these topics, so other kids can join us online."

"This is impressive," Mrs. Scott says.

"Indeed," Mr. Irving adds.

Ms. Paterson's face glows with pride.

Without mentioning Norbu, the quantum wearable, Zara's holographic existence, or the airship, our plans don't sound as far-fetched as I thought. So far, my parents haven't brought up our omissions. Being Anachronists, they're more open to ideas like time-travelers. I figure they know it's something we can't prove. They've never seen Norbu, and Zara isn't a show-and-tell sort of thing. Explaining a light blue holographic Saluki, without mentioning Norbu and explaining Chardin's Quantum, would be some kind of impossible.

"Please," Will says, looking around the room, "we know this is a lot to take in, but we truly believe that we have the power to make a difference. All we need is your support."

Just as they seem to be considering our plea, there's a buzz.

"I'm sorry," Dad says, removing his phone from his pocket. He's about to turn it off when a message catches his eye. "Good heavens! This is simply preposterious... The board has completed its review and exonerated Mr. Milnex of all charges.

"According to their findings, EverSave's recent activities fully align with the foundation's charter."

Mom's lips go tight, as she struggles to rein in her old-fashioned expletives.

"What about the evidence the children collected?" she asks.

Dad scans the message. "Apparently, EverSave was serving as an ombudsman, overseeing to ensure that such activities were done according to the law. The jaguars, it says, were being legally collected for zoos."

Sage jumps up and shakes her fist in the air. "What about the bee-killing pesticides?"

"As incredible as it may seem, those pesticides are still legal in some countries," Dad says, shaking his head. "However, I do not recall a clause in EverSave's founding documents that authorizes us to monitor and regulate actions that are at odds with our overall charter, to protect and preserve the natural world."

"Is there anything you can do?" I ask.

"I need to review the founding charter," Dad says, tapping his foot impatiently. He's eager to be off to his study to examine the documents.

Mom intervenes. "Let's take a break." She smiles, turning to the parents. "You've traveled a long way. Please help yourselves to some snacks and visit with your children. Let's meet back for lunch in an hour."

"Thank you," Mrs. Scott says, turning to Mr. Scott. "Let's take a walk, stretch our legs a bit?"

"The clouds look dark," Mom says, glancing out the window. "Better take a few rain nappers along."

Mr. and Mrs. Scott frown.

"Umbrellas," Mom hastily self-corrects, wincing at me.

Sage leaps to her feet. "Can I show my mom your amazing greenhouse? Please? She's going to love it."

"Of course," Mom smiles. "You'll find the Mackintoshes and galoshes in the mudroom."

The Irvings offer to help mom with lunch preparations. I'm glad they don't want to hang out with Jack because I need to talk to him.

My stomach feels queasy, probably from nerves, or too many cucumbers from the snack tray.

"How do you think it's going?" I ask as soon as we're alone.

Jack palms his face. "Terrible."

"Wait. Really?"

Jack nods. "Our parents work for EverSave. That's means they're indirectly involved in everything we saw. They must be furious."

"What's an ombudsman, exactly?" I ask.

"It's someone who investigates and resolves complaints of wrongdoing within an organization," Jack says with typical dictionary precision.

"That's convenient, don't you think?"

Jack frowns. "How so?"

"Chronnite set up a way to engage in illegal activities by using EverSave to cover their tracks."

"So you think it's a conspiracy?" Jack's eyebrows shoot up.

I nod. "Dad's memory is like yours—If he doesn't remember an ombudsman clause that's because it wasn't there.

"Wait, so you're saying . . . Chronnite somehow pressured EverSave to alter its founding documents as they did at Thistleton!"

"Exactly. Most likely Chronnite put some 'fund-raising' money in Mr. Milnex's pocket. I've never liked that man."

"Lexa, I think you might be onto something."

Sometimes I wonder how Jack can be so smart and miss something so obvious.

I glance out the window. The sky is dark gray, and the rain is coming down fast. Will's family rushes down the street, their vintage umbrellas no match for the windy conditions.

"Jack, I have a bad feeling."

"It's just a little rain, Lexa," he says, trying to reassure me.

But we both know we're not talking about the weather.

Chapter Three

The bad feeling stays with me throughout lunch. I wonder what Dad found out about the ombudsman clause, but mom wouldn't want to discuss Chronnite at the dinner table—so I fight the urge to bring it up and turn my attention to the conversation.

"Did you know that fungi are more closely related to humans than to plants?" Mrs. Scott is saying.

"For real?" Sage asks.

Mrs. Scott nods enthusiastically. "Fungi are a scientific frontier. Just yesterday, I heard about a company using the fungal kingdom to create palm oil. Imagine that!"

Mr. Scott clears his throat. "That would be Palmless. They aim to protect the rainforest from palm oil-driven deforestation. They're on our radar at Fidy," he says before being interrupted by the buzz of his phone. "Sorry," he winces, looking apologetically at his wife. "It's Flenoyd Preen. I have to take it."

Mrs. Scott sighs.

A few moments later, Mr. Scott returns, looking bewildered. "Flenoyd said there's a rumor our department is being shuttered—"

Mrs. Scott frowns.

"What? That's nonsense. Fidy is a world leader in sustainability initiatives. They have a thirty-year plan to green the supply chain. I don't believe it. Why would they do such a thing?"

"Flenoyd said Carbon Capture 360 is set to be repealed. Without that law, corporations don't have to deal with their carbon emissions. And departments like ours become an obstacle."

"Does that mean you're fired?" Will asks, a slight quaver in his voice.

Will's question hangs in the air.

An unpleasant feeling spreads through my chest. I reach for my locket and twist the tiny key that hangs beside it, trying to calm down. The grandfather clock chimes one o'clock.

"Uhm." Mrs. Scott clears her throat. "Son, I don't want you to worry about your dad's job security. Flenoyd Preen is a gossip, I'm sure it's nothing but a baseless rumor. And if it isn't," she adds, "I'll hire your dad to help me run the family mushroom farm. Business is booming, driven in part by sustainable packaging initiatives—"

Ring-a-ling.

The doorbell interrupts Mrs. Scott.

"Excuse me," Mom says, leaving the table.

Moments later she returns holding a box. "Did you order Welly's online?" she asks Dad.

"No." He shakes his head.

Mom is committed to supporting local businesses, so we rarely receive packages by mail. The boot-sized box is a mystery she can't resist.

"I hope you don't mind," she says to our guests. Before anyone can respond, she opens the box and drops it. Half a dozen bright green parrots spill onto the floor; their red crown feathers cluster together like a pool of blood in a green sea.

A collective gasp fills the room as everyone stares at the dead birds. Mom's face goes pale. Dad rushes to her side.

I recognize the bird as the thick-billed parrot, one of their favorites. They'd won a lawsuit against developers threatening to destroy the bird's habitat.

"Who would do such a thing?" Mom says.

"Someone who wants us to stop digging into EverSave's connection with Chronnite!" Dad says, between clenched teeth. "This is crossing a line. No one uses violence to threaten my family!"

Ms. Irving squats beside the box, picking up the dead parrots and putting them back inside. "There's a note," she says, handing it to my mother.

Mom scans the note and her face goes hard.

"What does it say?" I ask.

She shakes her head and passes the note to Dad.

"Lexa, take your friends upstairs," he says.

"But," I protest, "that's not fair."

I want to talk about everything that's happening. It feels like it's all connected —past actions to help the environment, such as lowering carbon emissions and protecting wildlife habitats, are being undone.

Is it because of us? To scare us or slow us down? Or worse, is it because we were supposed to do something already, and we're too late?

It feels way too important just to be sent upstairs while our parents talk. We're part of this, too! It's the whole reason everyone is even here.

"No arguing." Dad glares.

He's not budging, and Mom is frowning at me, too.

I turn on my heels and stomp from the room.

Meanwhile in the Future at G.A.I.A. Headquarters...

Chapter Four

"What in the name of the ten million things are they doing?" Pasha purr-growls, pouncing the moment I open my eyes. "Have they left Ferndale yet?"

"No," I sigh. "Things are unraveling."

"Unraveling, unraveling? Or unraveling as in a figure of speech?"

"I don't know." I exhale, realizing I've been holding my breath. "Do you know if Carbon Capture 360 was ever repealed?"

Pasha's eyes narrow. "Carbon Capture 360 was a historic win. Of course, it wasn't repealed."

"Well, that's a relief."

I have a sinking feeling inside. I can't risk accessing the Time Portal again so soon, so I'm eavesdropping the only way I know how—*dream-traveling meditation.*

Initially, my plan was to learn it to show Master Masayuki that I was qualified for advanced classes.

But that was before I met the shaman. Before I stole the Obscurer. And before I accessed the Portal.

Now it's better to keep my dream-traveling secret.

Dream-traveling meditation requires intensive concentration. It has drawbacks—it's time-consuming and nearly impossible to communicate with the dreamer, especially if you're trying to reach people untrained in altered states of consciousness, which includes nearly everyone in the past. The Portal makes things so much easier.

Pasha climbs onto my shoulder. "Why did you say that about Carbon Capture 360? What did you see? Are we in trouble? Are you going to be expelled?"

I palm my face. Pasha is pushing all my buttons.

"Why'd you have to go and say that?!"

She jumps off my shoulder onto the narrow sill of the large oval window that frames a breathtaking view of the mountains.

None of my friends have a window in their room—not that I have many friends. But still, I know I'm lucky. Most rooms are internally facing and, in general, windows are strategically placed and somewhat scarce—especially those as large as mine. I've never given much thought to my window. But the possibility of expulsion has made me appreciate everything more. I can't imagine living anywhere else. I glance around the small room, admiring it. To the window's left side, two bookcases are carved into the rock, boasting shelves filled to the brim with rare, old books. In front of the bookcases, a cozy futon doubles as a seating and sleeping area. A small rectangular rug between the window and sofa adds warmth to the room.

I take a deep breath, inhaling the fragrant air. My room smells of sandalwood, clove, cinnamon, and other warm and exotic spices that have infused every surface over the years. It's the smell of home—the only one I've ever known.

My gaze shifts to the bookshelf on the left and lands on the top shelf. Concealed inside a book with a hollowed-out core is the portable Quantum Obscurer. I did not damage the book; it was already defaced. However, I did steal the Obscurer. A far more serious crime. I press my knuckles into the back of my neck, trying to work the tension out as Master Reed taught in the Relaxation course, but the knots aren't moving.

"You should consult the mini quantum globe," Pasha suggests. "I know I said that Carbon Capture 360 wasn't repealed, but that was hopeful thinking. Check it!"

"You know I'm no good at it—it will just frustrate me. It's too small. I don't even know why they think we should be able to learn on it."

Pasha scratches her ear nonchalantly. "Go on. Don't act like you can't see anything."

I sigh. "Okay, if you're not going to stop bugging me."

"I won't." She flicks her tail.

The mini quantum globe—a quantum-infused ophthalmos, or eye stone—sits in its stand on my bookshelf. With a sense of resignation, I pick it up, return to my cushion, and sit down, placing it ceremoniously in front of me.

I roll the stone three times, a ritual to activate the quantum reaction between the bead and its stand. Instantly, a holographic sphere of light burgeons around the stone, teeming with infinitesimally small threads of varying colors and gradients, each pulsating with life and history. The globe's hologram showcases many layers, each representing different time periods, including today. These layers, with their pulsating patterns, signify the flow of time—brighter pulses for moments of significant change and dimmer ones for periods of stasis.

"Stop keeping me in suspense," Pasha hisses, leaning closer. "Are there any major fluctuations? Negative historical impacts? Can you tell if Carbon Capture 360 was repealed?"

"You know I can't see anything that specific."

But then, my eyes catch a striation of red threads, pulsating urgently—a visual scream amidst the calm. It's a spreading continuation, fraying at the edges, the red overtaking the green—a dangerous sign.

"What is it? Tell me!" Pasha demands, her eyes wide with concern and curiosity.

"Something bad is happening," I mutter, tracing the temporal markers with my fingers. These markers, glowing nodes along the threads, reveal snapshots of significant events. I pause at one, and the globe zooms in, revealing a fractal detail of the event's impact.

"They must have repealed Carbon Capture 360," Pasha concludes, her voice a mixture of anger and fear.

I sigh, tracing a line of light that flickers between shades—it's all connected—each choice weaves into the next, bound by the principle of interdependence.

I swipe my hand through the center of light, dispelling the hologram. Now that I've meddled with Time, I don't enjoy looking at the Possibilities as I once did.

"Tell me what you saw in Ferndale, please?" Pasha begs.

I pick up her tiny furry body and nuzzle it into the nape

of my neck, then I hold her up to my face and gaze into her silvery-blue eyes. "It's a long story—I'll tell you after class."

She hiss-breathes in my face like she's a miniature dragon trying to set me on fire.

"I'll be late." I wince. "And if I'm late, I'll have to stay after, and then your supper will be late."

She hisses louder.

I tousle her head, grab my cushion, and head out to my favorite course, Quantum Field Theory, better known here as QFT.

I pass the Ancient Bonsai and enter the Hall of Mirrors on my way to class. The thousand tiny mirrors with their kaleidoscopic reflections once fascinated me, but now multiply my guilt a thousand-fold. A thief, a liar, and a rule-breaker.

When I arrive, the Great Round is filling up with other agents-in-training. I place my cushion on the floor, equidistant to those on either side, aiming to maintain the integrity of the circle. I sit down and stare at a band of blue sky.

G.A.I.A.'s headquarters is ingeniously designed—the bulk of it carved into a remote mountainside. The fusion of stone and glass feels like one is living in harmony with nature.

I look around the circle just as Master Masayuki settles onto his cushion. We've always had a good relationship, but now I avoid his eyes like they're the Hall of Mirrors.

Master Masayuki is a Converger—one of the elite agents authorized for Portal travel. He knows QFT like the back of his hand. He doesn't waste any time getting started.

"Quantum theory," he begins, "is crucial for understanding the universe at its most fundamental level. Unlike classical physics, QFT sees the universe as a tapestry of fluctuating energy fields. It is a fundamental pillar in modern physics," he continues, "offering a comprehensive framework for understanding the universe's most minute components."

He gestures to the Quantum Globe, floating above us in the circle's center.

"These fields, manifesting as waves, form the fabric of reality, suggesting that every variation could potentially create a unique universe. This interconnectedness is central to our studies here at G.A.I.A. Who can explain its significance?"

I sit quietly, avoiding attention.

"Norbu," he calls, as if sensing my reluctance to participate.

I straighten my back and look at the Quantum Globe. "It means our reality is built on a foundation of infinite possibilities, stemming from quantum fluctuations."

"Exactly!" Master Masayuki nods. "Quantum physics challenges our traditional understanding of reality by emphasizing the inseparability of the mind and matter. This theory suggests that our consciousness intertwines with matter, shaping the physical world. This inseparability underscores the power of our thoughts and intentions."

He scans the circle. "Who can tell me what that means for us individually?"

Radhika eagerly responds. "It means that our

perspective shapes our reality. If we stick to a single mental framework, we are limited to a single outcome, which robs us of the vast potentialities the quantum landscape offers."

I catch Radhika's eyes; she's one of my friends. QFT is her favorite subject and we're in a friendly competition to see who can get the highest marks.

"Thank you, Radhika," Master Masayuki says, then stands, signaling the start of an experiment. The room buzzes with excitement. He lowers the Quantum Globe to our level; its glow illuminates our circle.

"Today's exercise demonstrates how intention impacts reality. Observe the Gaia Health meter," he says, conjuring a graph beside the globe. "It's at forty percent. Close your eyes, envision the color green—symbolizing renewal and vitality—and project this intention towards the Globe.

"Focus.

"Steady.

"Hold it."

This goes on for a solid twenty minutes.

"Now, see the results," Master Masayuki announces.

The meter has jumped to forty-five percent. Sounds of amazement fill the room.

"This is quantum entanglement and the observer effect in action. Our collective intentions were channeled to the planet and are reflected here on the Quantum Globe, proving without a doubt that we can manifest real-world changes—with thought alone."

He pauses.

"This works the opposite way, as well. Thus, this lesson

is not just about theory but about your responsibility as potential Agents. Reflect on this as you review chapter two for next week."

With a bow, Master Masayuki departs, leaving us to contemplate his words in silence. All I can think about is returning to my room to meditate my way back into Lexa's field of consciousness.

Chapter Five

"Whatever was written in that message sure spooked your dad," Jack says.

"Yeah, it feels like it's all connected," Sage says, echoing my thoughts. "EverSave's decision, Mr. Scott's job, dead parrots . . ." She twists her unruly curls. "I sure hope my mom doesn't get any bad news."

"I can't believe they are treating us like this! We know more about Chronnite than they do. We need to do something—now."

"Hum, Lex, probably need to wait until the storm's over," Jack says.

Sage whistles. "Those clouds look like some strange indigo tie dye, and they're getting darker and more twisty by the second."

"And moving unnaturally fast," Will adds, his eyes glued to the rapidly changing sky. "Looks like a tornado forming."

"Have you seen one before?" Sage asks.

Will nods. "Yeah, lots of them where I come from."

"Odds are it's not a tornado," Jack says. "Tornadoes can occur west of the continental divide, but they're usually weak and short-lived. I mean, we do get them, but it's rare."

Will glances up at the darkening sky. "Dude, if you hear the sound of a freight train—that's the sound they make—I'm telling you to take cover, somewhere away from windows."

Will uses his asthma inhaler. I wonder how many tornadoes he's been through, but I don't pry. Instead, I follow his gaze out the window just in time to see jagged bolts of lightning race in eerie patterns across the sky.

"Has anyone checked the weather report?" I ask.

Jack consults his device. "I'm not getting any signal."

We all try.

"Same." I look up from mine. "Let's head to the van and ask B.E.L.A."

"I don't think we should go out in this," Will says, staring out the window.

"There is an upside," Jack says. "No windows in the garage."

"Dude." Will high-fives Jack. "Now you're speaking my language."

We quietly descend the stairs and head to the kitchen to grab some snacks before making our way to the mudroom. The garage, which my family calls the carriage house, is a short distance from the house. We quickly don raincoats and run into the storm.

We're halfway there when an eerie sound fills the air.

"Run," Will shouts.

We race across the yard, the wind howling. I look back and see Sage struggling against the force of a gale. I grab her hand.

Up the street, a dark funnel cloud drops from the sky. An ancient oak tree splinters, and a car tumbles through the air before crashing down with a metallic screech.

"Hurry up," Jack yells, holding open the side door of the carriage house.

"Get in the van!" Will shouts.

We scramble inside.

"Are you sure it's safe here?" I ask.

"No!" Will shouts. "We're not safe anywhere, but this is better than your bedroom!"

"What about the living room? Is it safe?" Sage demands. But she doesn't wait for Will's reply. "I'm going back to get my mom."

"She would want you to stay here," Will says.

"I don't care what she wants," Sage shouts, now out of the van. "I'm going to get her and bring her in here."

"I'm going, too," I say, feeling the same urge

to protect my parents.

"Great, just great!" Will yells. "You guys are doing the exact opposite of what they would want you to do."

"Yeah," Jack says. "This is insane, totally insane. You guys better listen..."

But we're not listening because we're already across the room struggling to open the side door.

"Owooooo..."

A howl fills the room. Zara bursts in front of us, unbidden, barking and leaping, blocking our exit. The blue form of her body twists and turns so quickly it's a blur. She's in attack mode, three times her size and clearly trying to keep us from going outside.

"No, Zara," I say. "We need to go to the house to warn our parents—they're not paying attention to the weather."

Zara's bark intensifies, growing more insistent.

"What's she saying?" Sage asks.

"I don't know," I say. "It's hard to concentrate with a freight train piercing my ears."

"Try harder." Sage scowls, tightening her lips.

I close my eyes and focus my mind. "Talk to me, Z," I plead, trying to use our strange quantum connection to communicate. But I'm feeling rusty after six weeks of no practice.

And then, above the raucous, I hear her: "The only way to save your parents is to go. You must act fast."

"Well?" Sage demands.

"She says we have to leave now, or things will be worse for our parents."

Sage's face crumbles—it's the closest I've seen her to tears.

"I'll do whatever you want. It's your call," I say.

Sage closes her eyes to think. When she opens them, she's got her answer. "Zara wouldn't lie," she says. "Let's do what she said."

We rush back into the van.

"Let's move!" I shout. "B.E.L.A., get us out of here."

"It is not safe to go out in this weather," B.E.L.A. responds.

"I'm not asking! We've got to get out of here! Turn off autopilot. Who wants to drive?"

"Have you lost your mind?" Jack shouts.

"Move over!" Sage commands. "Our parents' lives are in danger!"

"So are ours!" Will says. "Can't you hear that sound? Didn't you see that car?"

"Zara said for us to get out of here, now!" I yell.

The eerie sound intensifies followed by a loud splinter as the double doors of the carriage house snap and fly off their hinges. A bolt of lightning darts through the room and then a deafening thunderclap.

"Go!" Sage screams, hitting the accelerator. Outside, sheets of rain and hail pummel the van. Debris flies through the air. The windshield wipers struggle to keep up with the downpour and the road is barely visible.

"Guys." Will's voice trembles as he points out the back window. "Look!"

The carriage house is a pile of rubble, but the main house stands untouched—as if in another time and place.

Sage has turned completely around. "I knew she was telling the truth," she says, a slight smile on her face.

"Hey, watch out," Will yells. "Don't you see that tree in the road?"

Sage turns the wheel, and swerves, sending the van into a tailspin before coming to a full stop in the middle of the road.

"Geesh!" she exclaims, and leaps from the driver's seat.

Will quickly takes her place.

"Huh, looks like we've got company," Jack says, motioning to a dark blue SUV that's tailing us.

"You think so?" Will asks, looking in the rearview mirror.

Jack palms his face. "Why else would it be out here in a freaking tornado?"

"They got lost and followed us because they thought we knew the way out of town?" Sage offers.

"Everyone who knows anything knows that you're not supposed to be outside during a tornado," Will says.

"Affirmative," B.E.L.A. pipes up. "We are approaching Russ Park. A detour onto a narrower forest route may help you evade the SUV."

"Thank you, B.E.L.A." I turn to where Jack stands studying the GPS. "Do you see the forest road on the map?"

Jack enlarges the map on the dash. "Yeah, it looks more like a bike path than a road."

Through the window, I see the local cemetery and recognize the trailhead. This was one of Zara's favorite places to walk off-leash. "We definitely shouldn't drive on this trail, it's posted no motor vehicles."

Will shrugs. "Uhm, I mean, we're already on it," he says, as we veer into the dense canopy of trees.

"We could turn around," Sage snaps. "We're going to kill the understory plants!"

"Look!" Jack yells. "It's gaining on us."

BANG! The SUV slams our back end.

"We need to do something! NOW!" Sage shouts.

"Like what?" Will says.

"Hit the fly button!"

We stare at her like she's conjured a magic incantation. We haven't flown since we arrived in Ferndale; my parents said it would draw unwanted attention. They made us promise we'd use it only in emergencies...

"Hit the fly button!" we shout in unison.

Whoosh! Materials transform, as the van begins to morph.

The SUV stops and two men jump out, running. One of them lunges at the van's retracting wheel, but in an instant, the transformation is complete and we're high above the redwoods.

"Looks like we lost them," I say, a mixture of relief and disbelief washing over me. Mom and Dad were right. Chronnite is after us.

Buzz – Ring – Beep – Ding –

Our phones sound, as if all at once our parents came out of whatever bubble they were in.

Around the airship, I hear my friends saying some version of what I'm saying...

"Yeah, we're okay, don't worry about us, it's

hard to explain, but this is something we have to do . . . Yes, we're planning to investigate the jaguars' disappearance . . . Yes, the ones in the video. No, we don't believe they're being shipped to zoos . . . That's right, we're headed to the Amazon . . .Yes, we know it's a large area that covers several countries . . . We traced the video footage to Ecuador. Of course, we'll stay in close contact. Try not to worry."

Sage falls asleep while face-timing her mom. I pick up the phone to close the call, but Ms. Paterson is still on. She asks me to watch out for her daughter. I promise I will.

I want to tell her that Sage usually saves the day, but it would only worry her to know the details. Plus, I've just lived through something between a nightmare and a miracle—I'm too tired to talk.

I climb into my bunk, close my eyes, and replay the day. One thing stands out above all the craziness.

Zara. She showed up.

Chapter Six

"Do you think she has a clue now?" Pasha hisses, pacing the table.

"I don't know—but at least she set out on the mission."

"FINALLY!" Pasha exclaims. "What part of the critical in 'critical missions' do you think they didn't get?"

"Okay, don't go getting down on them. They're just kids. They don't know the first thing about quantum distention."

"Why are kids so dumb, anyway?"

"PASHA! Don't say that. It's not nice, and it isn't true! Not even remotely."

"Well, I don't agree! You—I mean, we risked everything, and I mean everything, to warn them. And they just go sit around for weeks eating candy and popcorn! Meanwhile, forest fires are raging, glaciers are melting, and the big cats are dying off!"

Pasha is on a rant. "They have no idea! Absolutely no idea what's going on—what's going to happen!"

"Pasha, if they did, they'd just be scared. Maybe even paralyzed. And that wouldn't help anything, now, would it?"

Pasha doesn't agree. She thinks fear is a good motivator. I've never seen her so worked up, except when I came up with the idea to use the Portal.

"Settle down, Pash," I say. "It's been a long day. I'm beat."

Pasha leaps from the table and follows me to my futon. Before I can do my nightly meditation, she's curled up, asleep.

There's some truth to what Pasha was saying, but I didn't want to encourage her. I had no idea the kids would take a six-week break before setting out on the jaguar mission, but they really aren't to blame. They can only do what their parents let them.

I don't remember my parents, so I can't say much about parents or their concerns. Even Pasha says she doesn't know anything about my parents. One day I plan to ask Master Masayuki. Of course, that's if I'm not expelled. All I know right now is that using dream-traveling meditation to connect with the past is exhausting, though the upside is there's far less chance of being caught. So far, only the shaman has noticed me.

It's time to return to my meditation. Maybe Pasha will stay asleep long enough to stop bothering me.

I settle my mind and take a few breaths. One through each nostril to clear my energy channels. Then, I let my mind go empty—until it becomes an endless sea stretching out into Infinity.

Chapter Seven

"Uck! It's stinks in here!" Sage gripes, her nose scrunched in a knot. "Who let it rip?"

"Who smelt it dealt it," Jack chuckles, heading to the shower.

Our first morning in the airship is like an explosion in a stinky pillow factory.

"Hey, I called the shower first!" Will shouts.

"No! I did," Jack argues. "Didn't I, Sage? You heard me, right?"

"You all sound like three-year-olds." I grab the broom from the closet and pull out a piece of straw. "We'll draw straws," I say, breaking the straw into three sizes. I hold the three straws in my hand, covering the bottom portion so they all look the same size on the top. "Longest straw goes first."

My friends frown at this retro method of solving a dilemma, but they gather around.

Sage closes her eyes and concentrates hard, then pulls one. "Oh, darn it," she says, disappointed by the small size.

Jack chooses next; his straw is smaller than hers. Will is next. His straw is larger than Jack's but smaller than Sage's.

"I'm the winner!" Sage exclaims, dancing around.

When we escaped from Thistleton it had only taken us a few hours to arrive in Ferndale. We'd spent the time celebrating, exploring the airship, and eating all the snacks we could find. While I was home, I hadn't given any thought to what it would be like to spend days, weeks, or even months in the van. *Organization is going to be important.* While everyone else takes turns showering, I work with B.E.L.A. on an equitable rotation schedule, alternating mornings.

When we've all showered and eaten breakfast, we settle down to talk about our first mission.

"Let's give it a cool name," Sage says.

"What about Mission: Jaguar," Jack suggests.

"That's so basic," Sage frowns.

"Okay, put some ideas on the table," Jack counters.

We go back and forth like this until a familiar tightness threatens to take over my chest. "We're wasting time," I say, trying to keep my tone casual. "We're going to be in Ecuador before we know it. Let's just call it that for now—we can always change it later."

No one pushes back.

"B.E.L.A. launch Mission: G.A.I.A."

Our site appears. There's still a ton of work we need to do on it, but I navigate to HQ, select the jaguar icon, and open a folder full of the intel we've gathered.

According to reliable sources, it's clear that jaguars once roamed throughout South and Central America and the United States. The ancient Mayan and Aztec civilizations revered the jaguar. But over time, they lost habitat and were killed to near extinction north of the US - Mexico border.

"Looks like jaguars were protected as an endangered species in the US at one time, then lost protection, and after a few lawsuits, won protected status again," Will says, reading ahead.

"Like the thick-billed parrot," I say. "Developers have been trying to overturn protection since day one."

The heap of lifeless birds still weighs heavy on my mind.

"Yeah, they think they can scare us," Sage says, with bravado.

"Right, let's review the facts," Jack suggests, moving into detective mode. "We traced the jaguar footage to Ecuador, so we know Chronnite has some kind of operation there, but we don't know what it is, or why it involves jaguars."

Will scans the interface. "Primary reasons for capturing big cats, beyond sport, is poaching." He shakes his head. "Why would a corporation as rich and powerful as Chronnite be involved with something so sleazy?"

"What do you mean?" Sage scowls. "They're using bee-killing pesticides, releasing deadly chemicals, and clearcutting the lungs of the planet. You can't get any sleazier than that!"

"Right," Will says.

"Uhm." Jack clears his throat. "Let's review the jaguar footage and look for anything unusual."

It doesn't take long to watch.

"Anyone see anything new?" he asks.

"Just EverSave serving in an ombudsman capacity," I quip, sarcastically.

"Hmph!" Sage snorts.

"She just snorted." Will laughs.

"Hmph! Hmph!" Sage snorts again.

The boys crack up. Soon we're all cry-laughing and telling jokes.

"Hey, guys," Jack says, pulling a deck of cards from his pocket. "How about a quick magic trick?" He shuffles the cards expertly.

"Sure," I reply, still surprised by Jack's growing interest in magic.

"Alright, Lexa, pick any card you like," he instructs, fanning the deck out in front of me. I study the cards for a moment before selecting one at random. It's the six of hearts. "Now, show it to everyone, but don't let me see it."

I hold the card up for Sage and Will to see, making sure Jack can't catch a glimpse. Once they've both nodded, I return the card to the deck, which Jack promptly shuffles again.

"Watch closely," Jack says, his fingers dancing nimbly over the cards. With a flourish, he pulls a single card from the deck and holds it up triumphantly. "Is this your card, Lexa?"

To my amazement, it's the six of hearts. I can't help but laugh at the sheer absurdity of it. "How did you do that?" I ask, shaking my head in disbelief.

"Ah, a magician never reveals his secrets," Jack says, winking conspiratorially.

It's afternoon before we get back to planning what we're going to do on the mission.

"Let's dive deeper into understanding jaguars and their habitat," I suggest. "How about watching a documentary?"

"Can I make some popcorn first?" Jack asks.

"Make enough for me," Sage says.

"Me, too," Will adds.

I palm my face. The day is nearly over, and we don't even have the beginning of a plan. I try to hide my anxiety.

"Sure," I say, "I'll take some, too."

Ten minutes later, we're ready to start watching. We're immediately transported to the lush rainforests of South America where jaguars dominate the food chain. We watch a jaguar stalk its prey and learn about their extraordinary strength, agility, and stealth. The film also highlights other dangers of the Amazon, such as the Brazilian Wandering Spider and the deadly *Fer-de-Lance* snake.

"Whoa, those spiders are terrifying," Jack says, his face pale.

"Uhm," Will murmurs. "I'm more worried about the jaguars. They have the most powerful bite of any cat, a whopping 1500 PSI."

"1500 PSI is impressive," Jack says.

"And terrifying." Sage shudders. "Tonight, let's watch a documentary about Ecuador's flora and fauna. It's one of the most biodiverse countries on Earth.

"They've got everything from cloud forests to mangroves, páramo grasslands to Amazon rainforests."

"Sounds like one of us has already watched it," Will quips.

"Maybe," Sage grins, "but you haven't.

You're going to love it. They have kapok trees that reach to 200 feet. And incredible *bromeliads*."

"Bro, who?" Will jokes.

"Bromeliads," Sage says. "They're *epiphytes*, which means they grow on other plants without harming them."

"You mean air plants?" Will asks.

Sage wobbles her head. "Not exactly. Bromeliads and air plants are different, but come from the same family. The cloud forests of Ecuador are home to countless unique species, many of which have yet to be discovered by science. Can you believe it?" She beams. "We're about to step into a world filled with undiscovered creatures and plants!"

"Maybe you'll discover one," Jack says.

Sage blushes. "If I could stay there and live with the Indigenous people, maybe I could, or maybe they'd tell me about something only they know. They've spent countless generations living in harmony with the ecosystem."

"That's it!" I exclaim. "Sage! You're a genius!"

I reach in my pocket and pull out my phone. "We need to reach out to Indigenous activists in Ecuador and ask for their help."

Sage frowns. "Yeah. That's a no-brainer."

"On it!" I scroll through social media, seeking Indigenous voices speaking out to protect the environment. One account catches my eye – a young activist named Remi with loads of followers and strong community ties.

I draft a message:

"Dear Remi, my friends and I have discovered a serious threat facing the jaguars in Ecuador and time is running out to stop the damage.

"We need help from passionate local activists who know these lands and animals. With your expertise guiding our efforts, we believe we can protect these amazing cats before it's too late.

"Please advise if you might be interested in collaborating or can connect us to other Indigenous youth who share our commitment.

We aim to amplify your voice and follow your recommendations."

I read over the draft, hoping I've made it clear that we intend to support Remi's cause, not co-opt it. With a deep breath, I hit send.

I spend some time looking at Remi's posts and learn that she is an Achuar. With a bit more scrolling, I discover the Achuar are called the Dream People of the Amazon.

Goosebumps cover my body.

I feel excited for the first time since we set out on Mission: Jaguar.

Chapter Eight

"Act as a private investigator and help me find Anatola."

It's late in the evening when I overhear Will talking to B.E.L.A.

"Of course, where would you like to begin?" B.E.L.A. replies.

"I don't know. I guess plot Thistleton's campuses on the map?"

"Excellent idea. This will enable us to calculate the possibilities."

"Hey," I say, trying not to sneak up on him.

"Hey, Lexa, what's up?"

He doesn't seem to mind me being there, so I take a seat and watch the map materialize on the screen. Dots representing each campus are scattered across the continents.

"Did Anatola mention any campuses she wanted to attend?" B.E.L.A. asks.

"No," Will says. "I don't remember her saying anything about wanting to be sent anywhere. One day she was at Thistleton, and the next day she wasn't."

"Any unusual behavior leading up to her disappearance? People she interacted with? Anything out of the ordinary?"

Will pauses, considering the weeks before Anatola vanished. "She had written a formal complaint about the school's advanced surveillance system, and she was more . . . distracted, I guess?"

"Does anything else stand out, Will?"

Will shakes his head. "No."

Sage walks up carrying a snack tray. "You guys want some?"

Jack is close behind, ready to dive in. "What's up," he asks, pointing to the map. "Are we, uhm, planning to check out Thistleton while we're in Ecuador?"

"We are investigating Anatola's disappearance," B.E.L.A. replies.

"Oh," Jack says.

"Thistleton really is like a thistle," Sage observes, gesturing at the map. "It's blown seeds everywhere."

"Indeed," B.E.L.A. comments. "There are campuses on every continent. Would you like me to share more information about the locations?"

"Guys," Will cuts in. "B.E.L.A. is acting as a detective. Can we stick to finding Anatola?"

"Sorry," Sage whispers.

"Let's consider her background," B.E.L.A. says. "Where was she born? Where does her family live? Where did she live before attending Thistleton?"

"That's a good direction," Will says. "She was born in Florida. I'm not sure if her family still lives there, but that's where she was before she came to Thistleton. She talked a lot about how much she missed the ocean."

"Yeah," Sage agrees. "She was going to teach me how to surf, one day."

"Do you think she was sent home?" Will asks the question like it's a revelation.

"Being sent home is a distinct possibility," B.E.L.A. replies.

"I just don't think so," Will says. "I mean, if she was, why hasn't she tried to contact me?"

Sage nods. "Seems like she would have. It was more like, she just disappeared. Poof. Didn't even come back to our room to collect her things."

"Let's consider other forms of communication," B.E.L.A. says, resuming the investigation. "Did Anatola leave any paper trails, for example? Notes, letters, or anything that might contain clues?"

"Uhm." Will clears his throat, seeming embarrassed. "She gave me her poetry journal. But they're not clues. Just her way of expressing herself."

"Would you mind sharing those poems? There could be something within them that hasn't been considered," B.E.L.A. suggests.

"Uhm . . ." Will says, reluctantly. "I don't think you'll find anything . . . but okay, just a minute."

He returns with the journal and scans the pages into B.E.L.A.'s database.

"Anatola is quite talented," B.E.L.A. comments. "But I do not detect any hidden messages or codes in these poems."

"I told you. They're just poems," Will says, but he sounds disappointed.

"Let's continue the discovery process," B.E.L.A. says.

"Hey," Jack says, eyeballing the journal. "Can I take a look at that?"

"Seriously?" Will replies. "B.E.L.A. just reviewed them. They're poems, that's all."

"I don't want to read them," Jack says. "I want to examine the journal."

Will rolls his eyes. "Go for it."

Jack takes the journal. "Hmm," he says, "I thought it looked familiar."

Will shakes his head.

Jack grasps the journal in his left hand, pinches the top right-hand corner, and shakes it hard. When he opens it, color leaps off the pages—collages, bold scribbles, and drawings.

"What did you just do?" Will groans. "If you disappeared Anatola's poetry, you're gonna be so . . ."

Jack holds the bottom right corner of the journal and shakes it again. White pages filled with Anatola's poetry reappear.

"Wait?! There's two journals in one?" Will asks, flabbergasted.

Jack nods excitedly, "Yes! I saw one at a magic show. The real mystery is how Anatola made a journal like this in the first place. I mean, it can't be easy. She would've needed special paper and . . . I don't know . . . other special stuff."

"Now that we're talking about it," Sage ventures, "I remember her telling me she was a magician's assistant one summer. Helped someone in her family—maybe an uncle or a cousin?"

"Well, that helps to explain it," Jack says.

"Show me how it works," Will says.

Jack demonstrates the trick, and we all give it a try. When we've all succeeded at least once, Will excuses himself.

"I'll just go . . . you know . . . see what I can find out. Thanks, guys," he says, heading to his bunk to read in private.

Sage whispers in my ear, "Does he have a mad crush on her, or what?"

"Definitely," I whisper back. "I can't wait to meet her."

"Yeah, she's great." Sage smiles. "I hope we find her."

Chapter Nine

"What are they doing now?" Pasha asks, interrupting my meditation.

"They're looking for Anatola."

"Good. They're finally doing something productive. Did you see anything else?"

"Yes." My voice falters. "You don't want to know."

"What could be worse than the potential repeal of Carbon Capture 360? Without that law, we might've never been born."

"Kayou has been kidnapped!"

"No!" Pasha hisses. "Who would kidnap a shaman? Wait . . . Did he tell you that was going to happen?"

I shake my head. "No." A chill runs down my spine. "What if it wasn't supposed to happen? What if it's my fault?"

Pasha jumps on my lap. "I bet it doesn't have anything to do with us. I mean, you. No. Scratch that. Of course it does. Kayou gave you the critical missions. But no way the kidnapping's your fault. If I had one guess, I'd say it's because those kids waited around for six weeks . . . six solid weeks!"

"Pasha! Stop blaming the kids."

Pasha buries her face under her paw, pretending to

clean it. She hates to be reprimanded.

"If Kayou's kidnapping is anyone's fault, it's probably mine. I shouldn't have accessed the Portal."

"I tried to warn you."

I palm my face. "Yeah, I remember."

"You had good intentions, though." Pasha leaps onto a bookshelf so we're at eye level. "And it seemed to make sense—at least to you."

I bury my face in my hands. "Yeah, best-laid plans and all that."

"Well, so far, it's working. The Threads haven't unraveled and the extinction event was prevented—at least for now. And the Masters still think it's because of something they did."

"Yeah. That was yesterday. Today, the shaman is a prisoner. There's no telling what rips that will create. Maybe the last Thread will break today."

Pasha scrambles up my leg. "That's not how things work, and you know it. And even if it were, we're not going to let that happen. Are we? There are a gazillion possible futures . . . Right?"

I look into her pale blue eyes and get lost there for a moment. I wonder why she loves me so much.

"What do you have in mind?" I ask.

She raises her tiny brows. "Going back in time to investigate the kidnapping."

"Pasha!"

I can't believe my ears. She tried to talk me out of using the Portal the first time, the second time, the third time, and every time since. "You made me promise that I'd never do it again. Never-ever. Remember?"

"Yeah, well . . . I've changed my mind. It's generally against my principles, but I allow myself to do it, once in a great while. But if you get caught . . ."

"I know, I know—you had nothing to do with it."

Chapter Ten

"Guys, great news! I just heard from Remi!" I bound off my bunk. "She's invited us to stay at Kapawi Ecolodge! Says they're closed for renovations while they implement a new photovoltaic system."

"An ecolodge?" Sage frowns. "How are we going to save the jaguars by staying cooped up at a fancy hotel? We're supposed to be camping in the rainforest. Remember?"

"B.E.L.A., show us what you've got on Kapawi Ecolodge," I say.

"Searching the web," B.E.L.A. responds. "According to their website, Kapawi is located near the Ecuador-Peru border in the heart of Ecuador's most pristine rainforest. This remote region, called the Sacred Headwaters, is accessible only by plane or boat. It is situated on the Achuar's ancestral lands and owned and operated by local Achuar people."

"Wow, I love that aerial view of the lodge!" Sage exclaims, pointing at an image on the website. "It looks sort of like flower pods."

"Yeah, it's great..." Will adds, "But Ecuador is roughly the size of Colorado. Is it anywhere near our destination?"

"I don't know. I didn't share any precise mission details with Remi. I just told her we're concerned about a serious threat facing Ecuador's jaguars and asked for advice. This is what she's offering. I think we should accept. She says we'll be immersed in her culture and learn about life in the Amazon. It's a chance to get our bearings and hopefully make friends with some locals who are willing to help us."

"Let's map our destination against the Ecolodge coordinates and see how close they are," Jack suggests.

"On it," B.E.L.A. responds.

Two red locators blink to life on the map—one hovering over the Kapawi Ecolodge, the other pinpointing our true destination.

"Compiling coordinates," B.E.L.A. replies.

Will gives a low whistle.

"I can't believe it," Jack mutters. "Lexa, you have unbelievable luck."

Sage looks up from her sketchpad. "It's called synchronicity."

"Kapawi Ecolodge," B.E.L.A. says, "is an excellent destination. It minimizes the environmental impact of your visit, and its

isolation provides an optimal operation base to begin investigating the regional jaguar disappearance phenomena."

I look at the team. "So, is it a go?"

"As long as we get to camp outside under the stars while we're there," Sage says.

"Maybe they'll teach us how to avoid jaguars before we do that," Jack quips.

Will and Jack glance at each other. "1500 PSI," they say in unison.

I text Remi:

"Thank you so much! Kapawi sounds amazing. Invitation accepted!"

I add four smiley faces, four green hearts, and one Earth.

She replies, requesting our arrival details. A plan is finally shaping up.

B.E.L.A. sets our course for a remote location, about a twenty-minute drive to the airport. We'll arrive just before dawn, which is perfect because we don't want anyone to see the airship.

We spend the night packing and hanging out. Jack builds a map of Kapawi Village in Minecraft based on information available on their website. Sage shows off her sketch, trims her bonsai and watches *Flora and Fauna of the Amazon* for the third time. And Will sits alone, studying Anatola's journal.

"Find any hidden clues?" I ask.

"Nah," he says, "just loads of creative stuff. Check this out." He lays the journal flat, displaying a double-page spread filled with writing and doodles, some of it horizontal and some of it vertical. Some words are underlined, and others are boxed in. There are lots of spirals and circles. I feel dizzy just looking at it.

"What does it say?" I ask.

"Hard to explain—it's like she wrote down whatever came to her mind. But then there's stuff like this," he says, flipping the page and revealing a massive collage. There are stamps, stickers, random words, magazine cutouts, tiny maps, musical notes, and more.

Will shakes his head. "I just wonder if it means anything, or if it's just art."

"Art always means something—even if the person who's making it doesn't know what it means."

Will nods. "I guess you're right. Thanks, Lexa."

Something about our conversation makes me homesick, so I go to my bunk and call home.

Mom and Dad fill me in on the ongoing drama at EverSave. They've sued Mr. Milnex, and what's more, they, along with the Irvings,

Scotts, and Ms. Paterson, have filed a lawsuit against Chronnite to take back Thistleton. Dad thinks he's found a loophole in the corporate purchase agreement that might revert ownership to M.T. Allen's heirs. He never had children of his own, so they've begun searching. They aim to return Thistleton to its glory days as a green school *par excellence*. Of course, they must win the lawsuit first, so they're sort of 'counting their chickens before they hatch,' but they feel optimistic.

Before we hang up, they tell me Ecuador has forty-five species of *psittacids*, including parrots, parakeets, parrotlets, and macaws. Of the forty-five, two of them are only found in Ecuador, and they're endangered: the white-necked parakeet and the El Oro parakeet. The El Oro wasn't discovered until 1980 and is only found in the cloud forests on the western slope of the Andes. They encourage me to catch a sighting and to take lots of pictures.

They ask me if Zara has come around, and I tell them, no, I haven't seen her since the tornado hit the carriage house. They also ask me if Norbu or Pasha has made an appearance. No, I reluctantly admit.

I'm glad my parents saw Zara at Thistleton, otherwise they might not believe my story. But then, there's the van/airship—and the

wearable—I guess I've got plenty of evidence.

By the time we hang up, all I can think about are Zara, Norbu, and Pasha.

Where are they?

What kind of "Global Anticipatory Intelligence Agency" does Norbu work for anyway? If these missions are so critical, why don't they send him back to help us?

The feeling of tightness returns to my chest. I take some depth breaths, in and out.

Maybe they'll show up tomorrow.

Chapter Eleven

Pasha paws her face. "So when are we going?"

"I'm going alone."

Pasha jumps off the windowsill. "When do you leave?"

"I haven't decided. I need to check the schedule. I want to avoid traveling during Master Masayuki's rotation . . . I feel he suspects something."

"Of course he does. Last time he was practically waiting at the Portal for you to return. If I hadn't shown up and distracted him, it would have been goodbye, G.A.I.A., for you."

"He was on rounds, and you know it. Stop being so dramatic." But Pasha's threats hit hard, and she knows it. The Agency is the only home I've ever known.

"Stop biting your lip. You just said you think he suspects something."

"I had a dream—and I think he was in it."

"You *think* Masayuki was in a dream, or you *know* he was—which is it?"

I stare at the Quartz cats-eye beads on my wrist; they don't talk back like Pasha's eyes.

"I can't help you if you start keeping secrets from me. Now, can I?" she hisses, arching her back like I'm a barking dog.

"I'll tell you later," I say, grabbing my lunch and heading out. "I'm due in five."

"As if you've never been late." Pasha flicks her tail.

"I'm trying to be on time. Okay? Master Masayuki says, 'How you do anything is how you do everything.' Stop making me late."

"Fine," she hiss-pouts.

I grab my cushion and rush to class.

This is the first lecture on Anticipatory Thinking—and I don't want to miss it.

"Welcome to the intriguing world of anticipatory thinking," Master Arden says as I take my place in the circle. "I'm sure you've been looking forward to our namesake course since your acceptance. And for good reason. This course fosters a mindset that is proactive, imaginative, and resilient—qualities indispensable in a world where change is the only certainty—and crucial for an agent."

Master Arden has recently returned from a sabbatical. There were rumors that she disappeared while using the Portal. I can understand how that could happen to a beginner but not to a highly trained master.

"As you are aware," she continues, "here at the Agency, we use *anticipatory intelligence* to protect the planet. It will behoove you to pay the utmost attention.

"Unlike simple forecasting, which usually just extends past and present trends into the future, anticipatory thinking takes a more detailed and multi-faceted approach to what might happen next. It is about understanding complexities, recognizing patterns, and envisioning various scenarios that could unfold."

She looks around the room, staring briefly into each of our faces, then continues, "Rather than reacting to future events after they occur, it's about being steps ahead and preparing for multiple outcomes. This requires a blend of critical thinking, creativity, and agility. It's about asking, 'What if?' and not just, 'What's next?'"

'What if?' is exactly the question I should have asked before accessing the Portal—and lying to the kids. If they'd known I was a trainee, they might have thought twice before listening to me. Of course, Pasha's right, the Thread might have Unraveled. I wish I knew more about the Agency's criteria for accessing the Portal—like how they determine which events in the past they're going to delve into. And how they decide who to approach. They shouldn't make us wait until after we're selected to train as Convergers to teach us that stuff.

I'm struggling to concentrate when a loud gong interrupts the lecture. It's not a normal sound around here.

The gong sounds again, and again.

I look around and notice the same confusion on the faces of my classmates.

"Dismissed," Master Arden says, her firm tone cutting through the clamor. "Continue your studies independently."

Her face is pained. I have never seen her so visibly distressed.

My heart races.

Have I been found out?

Without wasting a second, I bolt out of the room, and sprint down the corridor to my room.

Pasha paces the windowsill.

"Do you know what's going on?"

She hops onto the table. "The quantum actuators are malfunctioning. They suspect unauthorized access of the Portal."

"Why do they think it involves the Portal? There's an infinite number of possible explanations . . ."

"Are there?" Pasha shakes her head. "I told you anything and everything could go wrong, but you wouldn't listen."

That's when it hits me.

The quantum actuators are malfunctioning!

Potential implications tumble through my mind.

Lexa's wearable might stop working.

If that happens, Zara can't help them.

B.E.L.A.'s intelligence might be compromised. And if that happens . . . the van will be at risk . . .

And Shamblin's gadgets . . .

"Norbu!" Pasha hisses. "Go tell the Agency's Masters what you've done. Trust me, it's always worse when they discover the truth themselves. Go turn yourself in—it will be easier for them to fix things if they know what you've done."

"Maybe it's not even related to me. Have you considered that?"

Pasha's sky-blue eyes turn cloudy. "No, and neither should you."

Chapter Twelve

"Almost there," Jack says, eyes glued to the navigation. It's just before dawn when the airship lands on a narrow road. We scramble out of the van, eager to look around. The stars are fading, and the first rays of light warm the sky. We make our way down the path toward the trees and, *whoosh!* the dense foliage bursts open, and a magnificent black jaguar explodes onto the path, bounding toward us.

No one breathes.

The jaguar pulls back hard, vanishing into the undergrowth in a fluid blur, gone as swiftly as it appeared.

I pinch myself, half-convinced I'm dreaming. "Did ... did you ... did you guys see that?"

Sage nods, eyes wide.

Jack's mouth hangs open, but no sound comes out.

Will takes one step backward and, in unspoken agreement, we step back with him. I expect to hear the boys quip '1500 PSI,' but they're speechless as we climb back in the van

and slam the door.

"To the airport, B.E.L.A.," I say, trying to make things seem normal.

"Oh my gosh," Sage gushes. "We just saw a jaguar! A black jaguar! They're totally rare!"

We talk about the sighting, but it's hard to find words to express how amazing and unbelievable it was. Something about it tugs at my mind—reminding me of a dream, but I can't remember the details. I promise myself I'll check my dream journal when we get to Kapawi.

"The airport is just up ahead," B.E.L.A. announces, interrupting my thoughts. "Would you like me to initiate parking procedures?"

"Yes, stop here," I instruct. "Park and lock up. We'll stay in touch."

"I will be waiting to assist you. Be careful," B.E.L.A. says.

We jump out, backpacks in hand, and make our way to arrivals where Remi, a tall, slender, Achuar girl, with long dark hair, stands holding a large sign that reads, "Kapawi Ecolodge."

"Remi!" I wave as we walk up to greet her.

"Welcome to Ecuador!" she replies, smiling warmly.

After introductions are done, she leads us to an airstrip, where a small charter plane waits to take us into the remote regions of the

Amazon. We climb in and strap ourselves to the worn seats.

The cabin vibrates as we take off, the ground slipping away. I press my face to the window, watching the Amazon open below. Brown rivers twist like snakes and the trees are packed so tight they look like a green sea. The clouds above are wisps, hardly there at all.

None of us are quite ready to land when we do. After profusely thanking the pilot, we follow Remi into the lush, green world of the Amazon.

The air is filled with chirps, howls, grunts, rat-a-tats, and sounds I've never heard before. I feel like I'm listening to a symphony, but I don't know the instruments—*living beings who are communicating in a language I don't understand*. More than ever, I wish I could understand them. As if listening from afar, I suddenly feel like Zara is walking beside me. I can't see her, but I know she's there. I glance at my wearable, but it isn't glowing, or making a sound.

"Wow," Sage gasps, pointing at an enormous tree before us. "That's a kapok tree... isn't it?" she says, looking to Remi for confirmation.

"Yes," Remi replies, seeming pleased. "The kapok tree is home to *Arutam*, the spirit of the forest."

"Up there!" Jack exclaims, pointing at the sky.

"That's a flock of chestnut-fronted macaws," Remi says. "Arutam is in the macaws, too."

From below, the birds' scarlet chests are brilliant. I fumble around trying to get a photo for my parents, but the birds fly on before I can. "Darn it," I grumble.

Remi laughs. "There'll be plenty of opportunities." Then she cups her ear. "Listen. Do you hear that?" She imitates the sound of a toucan with, "Grrunnkkt... grunnkt," resembling a combination of a pig and a frog.

"Grrunnkkt," Jack mimics. "Sounds like Sage."

"Maybe she's part toucan," Will says.

"That's not funny," Sage protests.

"Better a toucan than a pig?" Remi shrugs.

Sage laughs and we follow Remi until the trees open onto Kapawi Ecolodge, nestled in the rainforest.

"Welcome," Remi says proudly.

A wooden walkway is ahead, raised above the ground and appearing to float over the forest floor.

Remi leads us into the village, passes several round huts made of local wood and thatch, and then stops in front of one.

"This bungalow is reserved for you." She gestures to the right. "It has three beds and a hammock. I hope you can make that work."

"I call the hammock," Will yells.

"Ugh!" Sage slams her foot on the deck. "That's so unfair."

"Let's take turns," I say, trying to troubleshoot.

"We have a full day of activities designed to introduce you to our culture," Remi says, glancing at her device, "if you're up for it. You'll have to decide quickly—the blowgun introduction is starting right now."

"Blowguns? Too cool!" Will says.

"Yeah, I'm down!" Jack agrees.

"We'd love to join," I say.

Remi smiles. We follow her to a small clearing where several Achuar warriors stand, their blowguns by their sides.

Before leaving, she introduces us to Taku, an elder. Over his white shirt is a necklace of beads. He wears a headdress adorned with yellow and red feathers and has an ancestral pattern of black lines painted across his nose and cheeks.

Taku nods in welcome. "This morning, I will introduce you to one of our most important skills—the art of the blowgun."

He explains that traditionally, in the Achuar culture, only men learn the blowgun because they are the hunters. They are introducing this practice to visitors so that we can gain a better understanding of their culture.

"Thank you," I say. "We appreciate this opportunity."

He hands us each a long, narrow tube made from wood. "Watch," he says, holding the long, darkened blowgun with ease. "In your hands, you do not just hold wood, but a lineage of our ancestors—a lineage of patience and balance."

We gather around as he demonstrates the proper stance—feet grounded, body aligned, mind focused on the unseen connection between hunter and hunted.

"The animals we pursue," he continues, gesturing to the unseen creatures that call the dense foliage home, "are not just prey. They are beings like us, with families. For us to be successful we must live in harmony with the animal we hunt and with its guardian spirits, *kuntiniu nukuri*—the game mothers. We develop these relationships over the course of our lives."

As Taku talks about the spirits that reside in animals, I think of Zara. Our bond feels like something the Achuar would understand.

Taku picks up a dart, its tip sharpened to a fine point. "We hunt with respect, with an understanding that we take only to sustain our lives. We never take more than we need."

He places the dart into the blowgun and demonstrates the breath—the deep, controlled inhale, the precise aim, and the sharp exhale that sends the dart flying towards the target: a large leaf set up against a tree trunk. The dart strikes its mark, quivering as if alive with its own energy.

"Now, you try," he says, handing the blowgun to Will.

Will handles it awkwardly at first, struggling to mimic the balance between gentle handling and firm execution.

"Remember," Taku instructs us, "focus on your target and breathe steadily. It takes practice, so do not be discouraged if you don't hit the mark right away."

We each take our positions, facing the targets. I see Jack examining his blowgun with fascination, while Sage closes her eyes, taking slow, deep breaths to steady herself.

"Alright," I whisper, raising my blowgun to my lips. "Let's do this."

I aim, focusing all my energy on the target in front of me. With one swift exhale, I send a dart soaring through the air—and miss.

"Nice try," Jack chuckles, his own dart landing just a little closer to the target.

With each turn, Taku corrects our posture, guiding our aim, and teaches us how to breathe—the life force of the blowgun's power.

Eventually, our shots improve, from tentative puffs of air resulting in short, skittering flights, to more assured blows that send the darts further, some even hitting the leaf.

"Keep practicing." Taku's voice is calm and supportive. "With time, you will find your aim."

And so we do, firing dart after dart, each attempt bringing us closer to the mark. As the hours pass, our shots become more accurate, our breathing steadier, and our connection to this ancient art stronger.

When the lesson ends, we have a better understanding of the profound responsibility of wielding the blowgun, not as a weapon, but as a bridge between worlds.

We break for lunch and then it's time for our next activity: basket making. We gather around a small group of Achuar men who sit on the ground, expertly weaving delicate fibers made from palm leaves into intricate patterns.

"Welcome," says an elder. "Today, you will learn how to weave a *canasta*, as our ancestors have done for generations. We venture deep into the forest to gather materials, taking about three hours to create a large basket. You will be crafting a smaller one."

He hands each of us a bundle of freshly cut palm leaves and, together with his fellow artisans, begins to show us the techniques needed to create these beautiful, functional works of art. My fingers fumble at first, struggling to manipulate the palm fibers into the proper pattern, but Sage does it easily.

"Patience, Lexa," she whispers. "It's about learning the ways of the Achuar People, not a competition."

"Right." I nod, taking a deep breath. I follow the guidance with renewed concentration, carefully looping and twisting the fibers. As I work, I feel a sense of calm wash over me. The rhythm of the weaving slows my racing thoughts.

"Good," says the elder, observing my progress. "You are learning quickly."

"Thank you." I smile.

"Look at mine," Jack says, holding up a pattern of woven hexagons that will become the bottom of the basket. "It's not perfect, but it's getting there!"

"Mine, too!" Sage chimes, her nimble fingers working deftly.

Will holds up his basket, admiring his handiwork. "I wonder if you could make one of these from mushroom fibers?"

After the introduction to basket-making, a woman named Meena arrives to lead us to the garden. We walk through rows of lush vegetation and she explains how each plant serves a specific purpose—some for food, others for medicine, and still others for spiritual practices.

"Women are in charge of the gardens," Meena says. "It is an important responsibility." She glances at Will and Jack. "You are permitted as guests because you cannot understand our culture without understanding our deep connection to the garden."

"Thank you," Jack says.

"We're honored," Will adds. "My mom runs our family mushroom farm and I help out."

Meena smiles. "Our gardens, or *chakras*, are sacred and powerful spaces—the living spirit of *Pachamama*, our Mother Earth, resides here," she explains. "While we care for our plants, we sing songs honoring Pachamama's gifts and the nourishment they provide our communities."

Meena kneels beside a small tree with oblong leaves, its branches hung heavy with clusters of berries.

"This is the *Wayusa* tree. Every morning, our families gather to share sacred dreams over tea brewed from its leaves, in a revered ritual called *Hora de Wayusa*."

She continues, "We come together to interpret the visions and symbols that we have experienced in our dreams. The elders share their wisdom and ancestral knowledge, while we all offer insights into their significance and guidance. Some dreams contain warnings, while others may foretell an event or help us make sense of a current challenge in the community."

We spend an hour working in the garden, Sage is in her element, sketching plants and taking notes.

All I can think about is the dream-sharing ritual. *What would they say about mine?* I feel like, on some level, I'm always chasing Zara and, lately, Norbu.

After gardening, Meena shows us a few peices of Achuar pottery, with its earthy colors and intricate designs. She tells us how they collect the clay from the river and promises to show us another day. As the sun sets, we head back to our bungalow, exhausted.

"That's how Thistleton is supposed to be," I say, Plopping down on my bunk.

"Yeah, I know," Sage says. "That's because Thistleton's founder came from Scotland. The Paterson side of my family is Scottish too; we have a tartan and everything. The Scots were Celtic people who believed the plants and animals had spirits, too. Just like the Achuar."

"It's called *animism*," Jack says. "It was once widespread. And it's not just the plants and animals—it's the rocks, the water, the sky, everything. The Ancient Greeks were animists too."

"One day I'm going to Scotland to trace my family heritage and learn about the Celts," Sage says.

"Anatola's journal has Celtic patterns in it," Will says. "Maybe we can to go there together."

"Do you really think she could be in Scotland?" I ask.

Will shrugs. "It's on the list of possibilities."

"How many possibilities do you have?" Jack asks. "And what's the criteria?"

"Just anything repetitive," Will replies. Here, check it out."

While the boys try to figure out Anatola's cryptic clues, Sage and I go outside. She sketches and I check in on social.

As I scroll through my feed, I notice a post by Remi encouraging people to vote in an upcoming election and I share it. I don't know many people in Ecuador, but you never know who might see it—plus, I want to show my support. Remi's feed has lots of beautiful photography mixed in with facts and calls to action.

"Sage, did you know that Ecuador was the first country to codify the Rights of Nature in its constitution?" I ask.

"'Course, I did. Didn't you?" She frowns.

"Uhm, no."

"It was in the documentary. Remember? It said the Rights of Nature law included the Indigenous teaching of *sumak kawsay*—'the good life,' or 'life in harmony with nature.'"

As I scroll, I learn more about the history of the Indigenous people's fight to protect Mother Earth. "It's so inspiring!"

Sage nods.

A time-lapse nature reel catches my eye, and soon it's time to head to the Gathering Hut for a family-style dinner. We are the only guests, so we have a chance to get to know some of the Achuar people who own and manage the lodge. They greet us warmly, sharing stories and laughter, while introducing us to new foods like yuca, plantains, and guava.

After dinner, they invite us to the Hearth Hut, a larger community gathering space. A beautiful melody drifts into the room. Remi identifies the sound as the *quena*, an Andean flute. It sounds familiar, but I can't imagine where I could have heard it before. We sit around a small fire, basking in its golden glow.

"Friends," Remi says, turning to us. "I'd like to introduce you to my grandfather, Shakai, an esteemed elder in our community."

Shakai stands. "It is a pleasure to welcome you. Remi tells us you have traveled here on a specific mission. Please tell us more."

All eyes look at me—I suddenly feel young and afraid he won't take me seriously, but I clutch my locket and clear my throat. "We've come here to stop those who seek to capture jaguars."

I don't know how much to say, but this might be our only chance, so I continue. "We discovered video footage of captures taking place no more than twenty miles east of Kapawi, and we suspect it involves Chronnite."

A loud murmur erupts from the community.

"Our beloved shaman, Kayou Manish, has recently disappeared," Shakai says. "The area of which you speak is near his village.

"We believe his disappearance is connected to jaguar poaching."

A hush falls over the room.

"When he didn't return home, his family requested a police investigation, but none took place. We believe Chronnite is behind his disappearance and fear the worst. Remi shared your past activism against Chronnite, and we feel that your coming here now, at this moment, carries great significance.

"For us, the jaguar carries a special message: *touch your fears*. By coming here you have shown courage."

"The spirit of Arutam has called you in the jaguar's form. We are happy to support your mission."

Late at night, I lie in bed, tossing and turning. The words, 'kidnapped, shaman, and Chronnite,' repeating in my head. My mind races with worst-case scenarios. Shakai said the jaguar means to 'touch your fears,' but the weight on my chest feels heavier than ever.

Disappeared. Kidnapped. Fear the worst.

Why would Chronnite want to get rid of a local community shaman? Why aren't the police investigating? What are they trying to hide?

To quiet my mind, I replay the day. But I don't get beyond the first memory—the jaguar bounding out of the forest.

Shakai said the jaguar spirit sent us. That feels right. I think back to the jaguar fundraiser, where I first saw Norbu.

Was Norbu sent by the jaguar spirit, too?

No. That's crazy talk.

Stop thinking. Go to sleep.

Chapter Thirteen

Agency headquarters buzzes with activity. The corridors are filled with people rushing around. The mood is somber, one of intense concentration and focus. It's clear that something important is happening. I try to act natural while adjusting my tunic and entering the Hub.

"Did you hear about the quantum actuator?" The words drift from a cluster of agents huddled near a holographic display.

"This has the makings of a disaster," another voice adds, barely above a breath.

They don't seem to notice me. I pretend to check my wrist display, just a flicker of light and numbers, but I'm eavesdropping hard.

"Unauthorized access," slips through their guarded conversation.

"Can't be," someone mutters, shaking his head.

"Should be impossible," agrees another, "but the evidence . . ."

Evidence? What kind of evidence?

I edge closer to the group; the agents lean in, whispering.

"Excuse me," I say. "What's going on? I heard there's an issue with the actuator?"

Their heads turn, not expecting an interruption from a trainee. An agent locks eyes with me. I've seen him before, always quick with a command, not so quick with patience. He's sizing me up, deciding if I'm worth the breath.

"It's above your clearance. But it appears someone's been meddling where they shouldn't."

"Meddling?" My throat tightens.

"Nothing for trainees to worry about," another agent adds, her eyes softening a bit as they meet mine. "Just pay attention in QE—that is, if you hope to work here one day. You'll need a firm understanding of quantum entanglement for nonlocal objects. In the Schrödinger picture, the state vector evolves in time. In the Heisenberg picture, the state vector does not evolve in time."

"Right," I reply, trying to swallow my mounting alarm. "Thanks."

I've taught myself the basics of quantum entanglement, but I won't take the first course for a couple of years, or until Master Masayuki clears me.

They turn back to their discussion, leaving me battling rising feelings of guilt. *Did I misunderstand how the actuator works?*

I edge closer to another group of agents, their silhouettes tense against the humming backdrop of the tech-laden walls. One agent, a stern-faced woman, bites her lip and casts a glance at her colleagues.

"Listen," she says, her voice a hushed whisper, "there

are rumors of anomalies."

My pulse quickens.

Another agent nods. "The quantum actuator is the only thing that stands between us and the end of . . ."

"Don't say it," she interrupts. "Surely, no one would put G.A.I.A. at risk."

My heart plummets. I weave through the room, every step heavier than the last. Agents bustle past, their faces etched with concern.

I see Master Masayuki standing beside the Quantum Globe in the center of the room, his tall figure rising above the others. His fingers gesture with swift, precise movements as he analyzes the data streaming before him.

Pasha was right. I need to confess. This is my chance to make things right.

"Masayuki," I call as I approach.

He doesn't look up, his focus unwavering. I hesitate for a moment. "Masayuki, please. I need to talk to you."

Finally, he raises his head, sharp eyes locking onto mine. "Norbu," he acknowledges, his tone firm yet not unkind. "This isn't the time. We're dealing with serious anomalies. The quantum actuator's disruption could mean—"

"I know something about the quantum actuator and—" I interrupt, a reckless move, but desperation makes me bold. His eyebrows rise, a silent reprimand for my impertinence.

For a heartbeat, the world seems to pause, the room's ambient noise fading into nothingness. Masayuki studies me as if considering my words. "Norbu," he says, "you're bright, and you're curious, and you want to help, but right now, students aren't welcome here."

My heart sinks. Masayuki didn't understand.

I turn away and find a secluded spot, near a window. I stare out at the blue and take a deep breath, trying to steady my thoughts.

The quantum actuator has malfunctioned.

What does that mean, *exactly*?

How could it malfunction?

The only people with access are those who hold the Intention. That's its power. It's powered by the intention to protect all living things.

Did something go wrong in the duplication?

I need to contact Shamblin. If anyone has an answer, he will.

I need to access the Portal—*tonight.*

Chapter Fourteen

Howler monkeys are the first sound I hear. The second is Sage.

"Another dream?" she asks, taking a seat on my bed.

"Yeah," I say, closing the journal where I've been writing down everything I can remember.

"Did Zara visit you?"

I nod. "But it was all jumbled up and confused. It's hard to make sense of what she's trying to tell me. Or where she's trying to take me. Last time, I was chasing her..." I flip back a few pages and scan the entry. "Uhm... I was chasing her through Russ Park and the ground was morphing under me. Then I saw a jaguar and heard Norbu calling me."

"Sounds like she was leading you here," Sage says, as if it all makes perfect sense. "Tell me about last night's dream."

"Like I said, it didn't make sense."

Sage closes her eyes and waits.

I feel shy about the weirdness of what I'm

about to read, even though I know she won't judge me. I open my journal.

"Ahm." I clear my throat. "Zara is running through a sparkling expanse of sand—a vast desert. The sand is so white that, when the wind blows, she vanishes into the dunes, almost blending into the sand. I chase her a long distance.

"When I think I've caught up, I see a kitten. I think it's Pasha, but she isn't blue, she's white. She dissolves into the sand, too. I hear Norbu calling me, but it sounds like he's down in a well.

"I look down, and a well appears in the sand. Inside, it's pitch dark. I stare, but I can't see anything. The sands shift, covering the well. It turns dark and cold."

I leave out the part about waking up drenched in sweat. Somehow the dream doesn't sound nearly as terrifying as it felt.

Sage opens her eyes. "Wow, there were a lot of powerful symbols in that dream!"

"Really?"

Sage nods. "Yeah, but they say the most important thing about interpreting dreams is what it means to the dreamer. Do you have any feelings? What comes up for you?"

"I think it's just anxiety." I wince. "I'm all nerves about the missing shaman."

"Me too." Sage nods. "I had trouble sleeping."

"Trouble sleeping? Why would anyone have trouble sleeping?" Jack quips, sarcastically. "Come on, we're going to be late."

He hoists his backpack over his shoulder. Will follows on his heels, with an equally large pack.

"You guys are going to get tired of carrying that stuff," I say, sounding like a parent.

"Lexa, you never know when you're going to need something," Jack says.

"Yeah, yeah, I know the five 'p's'," I cut him off, grab my pack, and unplug my device. As I do, my wearable glows. "That's weird—"

"What?" Will asks.

"The wearable just—I don't know—glowed red. Only for a split second, but I've never seen it do that."

"Maybe Zara's coming back?" Jack says.

Will inspects the wearable. "I don't see anything. But we should probably re-sync just in case it was some kind of . . . you know . . . quantum update?" He grins and draws spirals in the air.

"Yeah, maybe Norbu's coming to help us find the missing shaman," Jack says.

"Or he's sending Pasha?" Sage suggests.

"We shouldn't get our hopes up," I say.

"Norbu said he wouldn't be able to check in all the time, remember?"

Will shrugs. "Yeah, but he didn't say we'd be investigating kidnappings, either. Did he?"

My heart sinks. "Listen, guys, I know this isn't what we expected, and if you want to..."

"Don't say it, Lex." Jack frowns.

"Yeah," Will adds. "We're a team."

"Mission: G.A.I.A." Sage grins. "Let's do it."

We extend our arms, placing the wearables in close contact. But the devices don't flash—

"Hmm," Will says, "that's not good. Let's try again later. I sure wish I could get my hands on one of their quantum textbooks."

"At least it's still telling time," Sage says, glancing at her wrist. "We're going to be late. Come on!"

Our plan is to meet Remi beside the *Pastanza* riverbank and paddle to the village where the shaman lived. From there, we'll head into the forest and investigate the area where the jaguar filming took place. It's all we have to go on, even though it seems lame.

"Hey guys," Remi says when we reach her. "I've got some bad news—I got word that a van was towed."

My heart races.

"What?" I ask. "Are you sure it was ours?"

"Relax," Remi says. "The local officials traced ownership to a guest at Kapawi, so they contacted me. Did you forget to take a parking ticket?"

My face turns red. "I don't remember seeing a parking..."

"They hide it well," Remi cuts in. "I should have warned you. Don't worry, I've contacted the facility on your behalf. You'll have to pay a fee." She winces. "But not until you pick it up."

I nod. "Okay, thanks for taking care of it."

"No big deal—let's go float." She smiles and gestures at the canoes.

But it is a big deal. Remi doesn't know the van can morph into an airship, or that Chronnite's henchmen have seen it happen.

Jack catches my eye. "Lexa, we definitely didn't pay to park. Towing happens. Relax." he says, stepping into a canoe.

Jack's usually the worrier. If he's not concerned, I must be overreacting.

I shake it off and wade into the water.

"Watch out!" Remi shouts.

A huge green anaconda swims toward me. Its camouflaged skin blends seamlessly with the murky waters and vegetation.

I scream, paralyzed with fear.

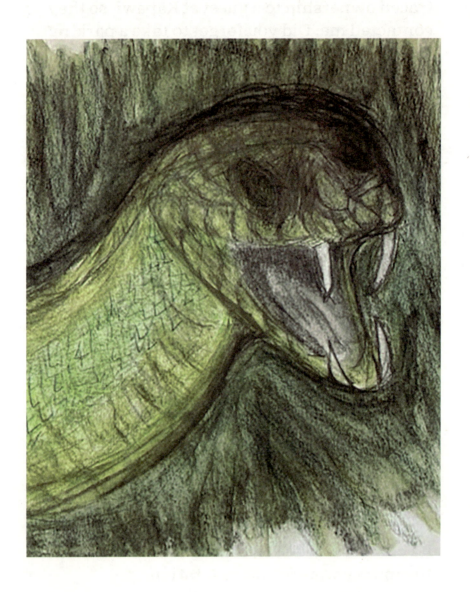

The anaconda strikes with lightning speed, its sharp, backward-pointing teeth missing my face by mere inches. Its hiss reverberates in my ears. I stumble, my legs turning to jelly, and fall backward into the canoe, my heart racing as the shadow of the massive snake looms over me.

Remi plunges her paddle into the water and pushes our canoe away from the riverbank. "Are you okay? I'm so sorry. We must have startled it," she says, her voice trembling. "But the fact that it attacked means it's hungry. You were lucky."

I nod, still in shock from the encounter.

We're only a few miles down the river when Jack dips his hands in the water. "Ouch," he exclaims, yanking his hand back. "What the heck?"

"Piranhas," Remi replies. "One bite is bad but keep your hands on the paddles and out of the water if you want to avoid worse!"

"Will do." Jack frowns.

"Look, over there," Sage exclaims, "pink river dolphins!"

Remi smiles. "*Boto* used to be common here, but climate change has reduced their numbers. Thankfully, efforts are underway to protect them. Have you heard about the Global Declaration for River Dolphins?"

"No," Sage and I shake our heads.

"A few weeks before International River Dolphin Day, something terrible happened in Lake Tefé in the Brazilian Amazon," she tells us.

"One hundred and fifty-four river dolphins died because an intense drought caused the water levels to drop and the temperatures to rise. Now, key stakeholders have endorsed the Global Declaration for River Dolphins. They're working to get commitments from fourteen countries to boost conservation efforts. Ecuador is one of the original signers."

Ecuador is lucky to have a youth activist like Remi. I wish I had her knowledge and confidence; listening to her makes me realize how much I have to learn.

"Caiman!" Jack shouts, pointing at the water.

"Stay calm," Remi yells, paddling closer. "Don't panic. A caiman won't attack the canoe, just don't fall out of the boat!"

I feel a drop of rain and then, without further warning, the sky unleashes a downpour.

"This is bad," Remi says. "Head for the riverbank," she calls to the boys. "The river swells quickly—it's dangerous."

I have some experience with paddling, but my stomach knots as I think about caiman and anaconda lurking beneath the water. I focus on following Remi's lead and paddle toward the riverbank. Up ahead, Jack and Will struggle against the rapidly rising waters.

"Just keep moving toward the riverbank; we'll find you," Remi calls.

As Jack and Will move out of sight, my heart pounds. Sage turns to look at me, her eyes wide with worry. My anxiety spikes. I grip the paddle and struggle to keep my breathing steady.

Chapter Fifteen

"This is rash," Pasha rants. "You're not thinking straight!"

"You were the one who encouraged me to investigate Kayou's kidnapping, remember?"

"I changed my mind," Pasha hisses, pacing the windowsill.

"Well, I haven't. I need to see if I can find him. And I need to find out if my actions are linked to the quantum actuator failure—and for that, Shamblin's my best hope."

"What do you think he can do?"

"If the quantum actuator is broken, he can fix it—he duplicated it, so he knows how it works. It makes perfect sense."

"No, it doesn't. Just because he was able to use existing materials to duplicate future technology doesn't mean he knows what broke, where it broke, when it broke, or how it broke!"

"Pasha, stop," I say sharply. "You're making things worse. Without Shamblin's help, I have no chance of fixing this. From now on, only talk to me if you have something helpful to say."

"Okay," she says, "try this: don't go tonight. You're too keyed up. The Masters will be on high alert, and the Convergers will be using the Portal to try and sort this out."

"I know all that."

"Traveling in muons must have made you lose like a trillion brain cells," she says. "You used to be smarter."

"Pasha, come on!"

"Okay, I rest my case, but I'm sure going to miss you when they kick you out."

I sit down and pull my knees up to my chest.

Pasha climbs up my legs and nuzzles her head against mine. Her sky-blue eyes look pale, like small moons reflecting a silver galaxy.

"It's not just about the shaman or checking in with Shamblin," I say. "It's about Lexa and her friends. It's her whole generation. We must maintain communication with them. They are the Ancestors with the ability to save our future! You know that!

"They're the ones who turn away from the industrial growth society toward a life-sustaining society. Without them, the Unraveling will break us down beyond the point that life can continue."

"If I've messed things up and something happens to Lexa and her friends, important possibilities will collapse. It's one of the futures the shaman saw—when they grow up, they will do a lot of work crucial to creating our future. If anything happens to them, I might not be able to communicate with you or use the Portal to travel through time."

"Maybe the Portal part could be abandoned?" Pasha suggests. "Has it ever really served anyone?"

"We used it to save the Thread, remember?"

"We thought we did, but what if we made things worse?"

"No." I shake my head. "Kayou told me that if—"

"Don't say it. Repeating it is dangerous. It will echo through the Quantum Field. It's a possibility that's against the Intention. Look at me," Pasha insists gently.

I meet her gaze.

"Your intention wasn't to harm. You acted with compassion. That's valuable here, even if the path you took was unconventional."

She may be right about my intention, but in hindsight, I can't believe I accessed the Portal.

Convergers have years of preparation. I don't know how they determine what they're going to do, or what they've done. We don't even begin to study the Portal and its Histories until *after* we're accepted for advanced training.

I glance at my bookshelves; my eyes stop on *Quantum Portal: Theory and Practice*.

I regret ever finding that book.

I never understood what the Masters meant when they said, "A little knowledge is a dangerous thing."

Until now.

Chapter Sixteen

The rain has stopped, and the humidity clings to my skin like a second layer. The buzz of insects fills the air; it seems like we've been walking forever.

"Shouldn't we have found the boys by now?" Sage asks, her brows creased with worry.

"I know the twists and turns of this river like the back of my hand," Remi says. "Unless something terribly unexpected has happened, they will be banked just up ahead."

Sage twists her hair nervously. "What kind of unexpected things?"

Remi shrugs. "If I told you, you'd only worry more."

Sage glances at me. I don't say anything because I'm afraid that, if I do, I'll get all choked up. Jack and I go back a long way, and Will is like a brother from another mother. If I allow myself to imagine all the possible unexpected things that could happen in the rainforest, I might get overwhelmed with anxiety. So, instead, I focus on putting one foot in front of the other and holding on to my locket. I silently send a message to Zara, asking her to do whatever she can to protect them from any potential dangers.

"Do you hear that?" Remi asks.

"What? The howler monkeys?" Sage says.

"That not howler monkeys." Remi frowns. "That's laughter!"

I burst into a grin and Sage and I take off running toward the sound.

The boys are as happy to see us as we are them. They lose no time telling us about piranhas sloshing into their canoe, how they nearly tipped over, and how they were encircled by three caimans. It sounds like tall tales, but their expressions are genuine and, for the moment, I'll happily believe anything.

The sun slowly descends behind the towering trees, painting the sky in hues of orange and pink. We arrive at the Achuar village and are greeted by a group of young activists who have gathered to meet us. Remi introduces us and, as the night falls, we form a circle and our conversation turns to the plight of the jaguar and the shaman's disappearance.

One by one, they tell stories about Kayou. Most of them have been cured by him, or have relatives who have been. People travel great distances to seek his healing—they say he's a shapeshifter, able to see through the eyes of the animals and even spirits. In addition to being a shaman, we learn that Kayou is also a well-known conservationist and an outspoken advocate for the rainforest. He exemplifies the spirit of the Achuar people as forest guardians. His sudden disappearance has shocked the village.

I find myself holding my locket and thinking of how I felt the night Zara disappeared. I was frantic with worry, fearing for her safety. Although it's a very different situation, inside I feel like I have some understanding of the worry and anxiety they are feeling. When you love someone, you feel protective toward them.

As the night wears on and the fire dims, a young Achuar activist named Taish gestures to the west. "Beyond the river, where the jaguars once roamed freely, there lies a cavern-like building," he starts, his voice barely audible over the chorus of cicadas. "It's shrouded by the thickest part of the forest, and masked by tangled vines. We call it Death Cavern—jaguars who go in, don't come out."

Taish shares the coordinates and what he knows about Chronnite's poaching activities.

It's a lot to take in. Jack palms his face. Will stares into the fire, then turns to use his asthma inhaler. He hasn't needed it on this trip until now. The smoke must be too much for him.

Sage draws patterns in the ash, wipes them away, and starts over.

Taish brings the quena to his lips and, softly, the plaintive notes of the Andean flute take their place among the night symphony of the Ecuadorian rainforest. Their melody joins the calls of endless frog species, the buzzing of countless insects, and the myriad cries of nocturnal birds.

In a hammock, under the stars, I listen to the now distant melody and retrace the day. The eyes of the green anaconda latch onto me. I was too scared to think of anything at the time, but now, all I can see is Norbu being attacked by a similar-looking snake in the airship—the last time we saw him. A bizarre feeling crawls over my body.

Has he been here before?

Was the incident in the airship the past, present, or future?

I'm tired. Too tired to think about this anymore. Tomorrow is a big day.

And the most dangerous of our mission.

Chapter Seventeen

We crouch behind a thicket of dense foliage, not far from the coordinates Taish shared with us. It's hard to see anything, much less a building.

"Are you sure we're at the right place?" I whisper to Jack.

He nods and points to a location on the map displayed on his device.

I notice Will pulling out a small drone from his backpack. "This is one of Shamblin's," he says. "Let's see what we're up against." His fingers fly over the controls, and in seconds, the soft hum of tiny rotors fills the air. "Drone's up," he whispers, eyes glued to the display.

The drone ascends, its hum merging with the jungle's sounds, a barely visible speck in the busy rainforest canopy. Will scans the display, his eyebrows furrowed in concentration. "Got it," he says suddenly, tapping the screen. "One guard. Stationed outside what looks to

be the main entrance."

I edge closer, peering over his shoulder.

"He's packing heat," Will says.

Jack frowns. "It's Chronnite, of course he is."

"Any cameras?" I whisper.

"Scanning," Will replies. "Shh . . . he's taking a call . . ." A few moments later, he reports, "They've caught a big cat. And they're bringing it in."

A feeling of outrage surges through me. "We'll catch them in the act."

"Remember," Jack whispers. "We're here to collect evidence to share with the police. Not to get killed."

"They've arrived," Will says. We look at the display and see two men step out of a small truck. They uncover a large cage in the back. Inside it, a jaguar lies on its side. Blood drips from the cage, but the jaguar lifts its head slightly—it's still alive.

Anger floods my body. Anger I haven't felt since the night Zara was hit. I flashback to that moment, her body lying helpless on the side of the street.

"We've got to save it," I say, looking at my friends.

Jack nods. "We will. Let's just stick to the plan."

"No. We need to get the jaguar out alive—now!"

Will speaks softly. "If we wait until the poachers leave, it'll be four against one."

Jack agrees. "As soon as they leave, I'll create a distraction and we'll slip in, collect the evidence, and free the jaguar."

My eyes never leave the jaguar. My breathing is erratic. I feel like I'm inside the jaguar's mind.

Sage takes my hand. "Breath with me . . ." she says, gently. "We're going to make it right. Let's get centered. Get calm. Focus."

I take a few breaths, but all I can think about is the jaguar. I look at Sage. "They might kill it while we're out here breathing, waiting to get past the guard. Did you think about that? I can't live with that!"

Sage exhales, low and slow. "You're right. Let's do it."

I turn to Will and Jack. "Sage and I are going in."

"Lex," Jack says, "we're all going in . . . together . . . in just a few moments, remember?"

I shake my head slowly. "No, things have changed. We came to get evidence, but now a jaguar's life is at risk. Taish said they call it the death cavern . . . what goes in doesn't come out."

Jack and Will glance at each other and nod in agreement.

"Okay, but let's stay level-headed," Jack says.

He reaches into his backpack and removes a small remote-controlled vehicle and a round object that looks like a yo-yo. "This will grab their attention."

"Well, that was fast," Will says, gesturing at the display. The poachers are driving away.

"Oh no . . ." I groan. "What if they . . ."

"Come on," Jack whispers, clipping the contraption to the back of the remote-controlled vehicle, and driving it the opposite direction while we creep toward the cave entrance. When the RC's in place, he presses a button and detonates it. There's a loud bang, followed by another.

The guard startles, then darts toward the source of the commotion, leaving his post unguarded.

We race through the forest, reach the entrance, and slip inside the door.

"Lock it," I scream, heart racing.

"Done," Jack breathes.

A sloped walkway descends into a large, cavernous room. It's pitch dark, but I don't need light. I'm pulled toward the jaguar by its heartbeat.

"Follow me," I say, moving toward the sound, which is amplified in my ears. Each step feels like forever as I navigate by an inner knowing, wandering down a dark hallway, turning left and right, again and again, as if I'm inside a nightmare's labyrinth.

Deep inside, we find the cage. The jaguar is lying inside, its breathing labored. We squat down beside it.

"It's just a cub," Sage whispers.

I nod. "We've got to get help—fast."

"First, we'll need to find our way out of here. I feel like a rat in a maze," Sage says.

"Yeah, Chronnite's maze," Will says, palming his face.

I had found my way to the jaguar by some deep intuitive field, but I didn't know how to find the way out. I'm reluctant to leave the jaguar's side, but we need to find an exit before the guard catches us.

"I memorized the turns, but we need more light," Jack says, sending a beam around the room using his device. The others pull out their devices and do the same.

In the dim light, we see several computers and multiple screens. Against the wall is a long table with a full-scale replica of a large city. Every detail is meticulously crafted to scale—office buildings, parking lots, fast-food restaurants, even cars.

"Looks like a data hub," Will whispers, gesturing to the computers. "The technology is a bit outdated, though." He runs his fingers over the keys.

"We need to gather evidence," I say. "Something we can share with the police to get this place shut down."

"I'm on it," he says, entering a string of code.

Within moments we hear a robotic voice.

"Welcome to O.M.E.N," the voice says as the display lights up, revealing several surveillance feeds.

"Isn't that the name of a old horror movie?" Sage asks."

"Yeah," Will nods.

Sage shivers. "I hate this creepy place."

On the screen's upper right, a live stream shows the guard outside, scrolling his phone. Other feeds offer different rooms. Will selects the screen on the upper right and rewinds the footage. We see ourselves sneak inside the building; we see the jaguar poachers exit; we see them enter carrying the caged jaguar. It feels strange to watch things move backward in time.

"Someone's sleeping on the job," Jack says.

I hold my wearable over the screen, but it doesn't so much as blink. "Yeah, and his name is Norbu," I say, increasingly frustrated with Norbu and his nonfunctional high-tech device. I open video record on my phone. "Can you go back to the part where the poachers are carrying in the cage?"

"Sure," Will says, pressing a key. But when the video resumes, it's wound back further than intended and we see a group of people entering the building.

"Are all those people involved in poaching jaguars?" Sage asks.

"I bet it's a criminal syndicate," Jack says, glancing at Will.

Will nods. "Those dudes look like SPECTRE and Maggia rolled into one."

"And with a name like O.M.E.N.," Sage adds.

"Let's see what else we can find," Will says, switching to another video, a recording of an event in a different room with a similar timestamp.

In the scene, a bald, stocky man approaches a podium. Behind it a large screen reads, "Planning The Future Together."

As he turns to face the audience, a chill run down my spine.

"Mr. Milnex!" Jack and I exclaim in unison.

"The creep who works at EverSave?" Sage asks, her eyes wide.

We nod.

"Welcome," Mr. Milnex says. "I have the great honor of introducing Chronnite's founder, Mr. Dominic Grimshaw."

Applause fills the room as a gaunt man in a dark suit appears on the screen behind Mr. Milnex.

"Welcome to the City of the Future," Grimshaw says. "While the future we're developing in your region may seem distant, it arrives even as we speak. Your children and grandchildren will benefit from the work we accomplish together."

As he speaks, his face is replaced by a series of images. Maps, architectural blueprints, high-rise condominiums, parking lots, fast-food restaurants, and well-known logos.

"We are up against some resistance," he continues. "From tree-hugging environmentalists who want to change the very definition of progress. Ha! Do they think people want to live in trees? Give up streaming and start farming?

"No! They want cozy recliners, fast food, and a good scare. It's up to us to provide for their needs."

Grimshaw's face hardens.

"We will not permit these so-called 'forest guardians' and their granola-crunching allies to destroy two centuries of progress!"

"We will not permit you to destroy our home!" booms a voice from the audience. The camera pans to his face—it's the shaman, Kayou Manish.

On the screen, Grimshaw laughs scornfully. "It looks like we have an uninvited guest. Who would like to escort him out?"

Two guards appear from the shadows and seize Kayou.

"The rainforests are the planet's lungs," Kayou shouts. "The only benefits your grandchildren will reap are smog, depression, and shortened lifespans!"

Will toggles between the feeds. On another screen, Kayou struggles to break free of the guards, but they grip him tightly and punch him until his body is limp. They drag him out of the room and into the hall, where the surveillance footage ends.

We look at each other, horrified. "That proves it," Jack says. "Chronnite is a criminal organization."

I nod. "We can give this recording to Remi, and they can use it to prove to the police that Kayou was last seen with Chronnite's guards."

Jack motions to the feed where the "Planning the Future" presentation is still underway. "Can I take a look at those maps?"

"Sure," Will says, moving over.

Jack toggles back and forth between the maps. "Wait a minute . . ." he says, his eyes shifting between them. "Guys," he breathes, motioning to the screens. "This is where we are now."

He hovers over the image of Chronnite Ltd. on the map. "Over here"—he navigates over the map—"is the rainforest."

He moves to a second screen. "On this map, Chronnite is here, but the rainforest is here."

"No, it isn't." Sage shakes her head, a wild look in her eyes. "That's a park. See, it says, 'City Park,' right there."

"I'm telling you," Jack argues. "That's what's left of the rainforest in twenty years."

"No!" Sage shouts. She runs across the room, climbs on top of the table, and stomps the model city flat. "No! No! NO!"

A beam of light falls on her.

"Oh no, you don't!" a deep voice bellows. The security guard flips a switch, flooding the room with light. "Kids?! What are you doing in here?"

"You kids are breaking and entering—and destroying private property, that's against the law."

"So, call the police," Sage blurts.

He raises his eyebrows. "You'd like that, wouldn't you? Around here, I *am* the police." He smirks, resting his hand on his holster.

"No, you are a poacher," I say, my voice trembling.

He scratches his head. "Nah. I guard the prizes." He kicks the cage, in a sudden rage.

The jaguar momentarily rouses, lifts its head and opens its eyes.

We connect. *I see you. I'm going to help you.* It's like I'm talking to Zara. And deep inside, I know the jaguar understands.

Anger swells inside me. In a swift move, I hunch my head and run at the guard, plowing my shoulders into his stomach and reaching down to pick up his right knee, forcing him backward—Dad taught me that a person can't go backward on one leg. The guard falls splat on his back. I jump on his chest and stomp as hard as I can. He grabs my ankle and pulls me down. Jack, Will, and Sage jump in, but he's pulled his gun.

"No one moves," he commands. "Or else."

I look at my friends and see the same fear in their faces. Chronnite's got us. We're trapped.

The guard trains his gun on us and sneers, threateningly. A muffled sound wafts in from outside and grows louder. It's the sound of voices chanting . . . one voice rises above the others. It's Remi!

"Protect Our Wildlife." Remi yells, rallying the crowd and urging them to stand against Chronnite.

The sound grows louder and closer—they've entered the building.

"Help!" Sage shouts at the top of her lungs. "He's trying to kill us!"

Remi and her friends rush into the room. The police are close behind them. They had arrived to disperse the protesters, but now they turn their attention toward the guard.

We huddle with Remi around the jaguar's cage and share the news of our filmed video footage—in whispers, we tell her about Kayou and the future city Chronnite plans to build. She doesn't trust sharing anything with the police just yet. They didn't come to rescue anyone, that's just how it looks on the surface. We exchange nervous glances.

"But they can't ignore the jaguar poaching—it's illegal," Remi adds. "And the evidence is gut-wrenching."

"Really?" I ask. "Do you think one jaguar is enough to prove what they've been doing?"

Remi frowns. "You guys haven't looked around. Come on..." she says, taking my hand and pulling me to my feet.

She leads us out of the room, into a now well-lit hallway. After a series of twists and turns we arrive in a large room. Under the lights, we see the room's perimeter is lined with tables covered with jaguar parts. Skulls, claws, and teeth all piled up—jaguar skins hang between the tables. I feel dizzy and sick to my stomach.

"Come on, you need some air," Remi says.

"No," I wipe my eyes and shake my head. "I need to stay with the jaguar until help comes."

Remi nods.

The police ask us a series of questions and take photographs. Jack and Will record everything—in case they decide to bury the investigation alongside Kayou's disappearance.

Eventually, the veterinarian arrives. She says she's seen cases like this before and assures us the jaguar will survive. She works with *Panthera*, an organization focused on helping jaguars, and explains that when the cub is healthy, they will rehab it and return it to the forest.

We exchange contacts, and she invites us to come watch the jaguar's release.

Outside, more police officers have arrived. A few have joined the protesters and carry signs reading "Nature's Rights are Constitutional," "Chronnite is Destroying Our Future," and "Stop the Poaching!"

After the protest, Remi walks us back to the village. That night, we go over the day's events. She explains that she'd had a particularly disturbing dream the night before. When she shared it during *Hora de Wayusa*, the elders interpreted it as a call for her to support us. Remi said she'd wanted to stage a protest outside the cavern for many months and felt this was the moment.

"Your timing was perfect," Jack says, with a silly smile.

"I'm glad it worked out." Remi smiles back. "You all got evidence linking Chronnite to Kayou's disappearance. It may be enough to get the police to search for him.

I spoke to the community, and the elders would like to invite you all to join us for *Hora de Wayusa* tomorrow—if you'd like to come."

I nod excitedly.

The morning dream-sharing is something I'd hoped to experience.

Chapter Eighteen

Pasha sits on the bookcase, staring me down. "Return the Quantum Obscurer and turn yourself in. They won't expel you if you do that. The Code is all about forgiveness and compassion."

"You mean the Code I vowed to uphold? *That code*?"

She twitches her ears and swishes her tail.

"The books are full of Agents' transgressions, and the forgiveness afforded them," I say. "But trainees? No. One or two mistakes, and you're out. Listen, I'm not going to debate this with you. Move, or no snacks tonight."

Pasha has curled up on the hollowed-out book, pretending to nap. I gently pick her up and place her on a pillow. The book is lightweight; I open it and remove the portable Quantum Obscurer—a device capable of altering muon signatures produced during travels. The device that renders my trips untraceable.

At its core, the Obscurer houses a miniaturized quantum processor and operates on a principle known as quantum interference. It creates a precisely calibrated field that disrupts the coherence of muon particles, preventing them from forming a detectable signature. Instead of altering the muons' properties, an additional quantum field is superimposed to cancel out their patterns, like noise-canceling headphones.

It's powered by a rare, compact energy source that requires recharging only once per decade, making it incredibly efficient. The creator, a figure shrouded in mystery within the Agency, designed the Obscurer for emergency use.

If this isn't an emergency, I don't know what is.

Pasha raises her head. "How long are you going to be gone?"

"Overnight. I'll find Kayou, then visit Shamblin. I'll be back in time for class."

"If something happens while you're gone . . ." She pauses. "Will we still be able to communicate, you know, like Lexa and Zara?"

My heart melts. I cross the tiny space and scoop her up.

"I think so," I say. "But you're not going to die while I'm gone." She paws my face. "No, I'm not going to die, either."

Chardin's Quantum. Pure love—an energy so powerful it can alter consciousness itself.

I had no reason to study it until Zara appeared—*a quantum possibility I never imagined.* How Zara used the minuscule quantum resonance manifestor in the wearable to make her benevolent signature visible in muons is still a mystery. Here, the Masters use massive QRMs to facilitate such communications, or at least that's what I've read. I've never actually seen the Masters using them firsthand.

I snuggle Pasha. "I'm coming back. You can count on it. Take a nap and let me prepare. You know how tedious it is for me to get in the quantum state of mind."

I light my favorite incense and move to my cushion to prepare for my trip through the Portal.

The first order of business is meditation. Everything about the quantum realm requires precision, but time travel takes that to its zenith. When I enter the Portal, I must manipulate quantum probabilities, using my mind to select the desired trajectory through the quantum-entangled pathways the Portal generates. Otherwise, I risk entanglement with particles from different times. If I lose quantum coherence, my wave function could collapse into an unintended era. I need to gather more information about Kayou's whereabouts; otherwise, I might lose my way.

I settle deeper into the cushion, feeling its support against my sit bones. I let my spine lengthen, imagining myself growing taller with each subtle shift of my posture. The tension in my shoulders ebbs away as if sinking into the floor beneath me.

Inhale. The fragrant air fills my lungs. Exhale. Warmth floods out. In this breath cycle, I find the rhythm—the heartbeat of my meditation. The world falls away with each inhalation, every exhalation. My senses sharpen, not to the room, but inward, where a vast landscape stretches out before me. I hold the singular intention to communicate with Kayou—asking him to join me in the quantum field of all possibilities.

My heartbeat slows, syncing with the pulse of the unseen world that throbs just out of sight. There's a tingling at the back of my neck. The energy shifts. It's him. I can't see or hear him, but I sense Kayou's consciousness, as real as the ground beneath me.

I relax more deeply into the Opening, hear chanting, and find myself hovering in a small, dark room.

"Norbu," Kayou says, acknowledging my presence. "They intend to make this my grave."

"We won't let that happen. Everyone is looking for you. I'm porting tonight; show me where you are."

As a door opens, a beam of light floods into the cell. I spot a small window with metal bars. For a split second, I see Kayou's body—badly beaten and bruised, his hands bound.

"Stop chanting," a voice yells, slamming Kayou with a heavy club.

The violent force shocks me, severing our connection.

I open my eyes, my heart racing.

I don't have the shaman's precise location, but I'm determined to find him. I straighten my tunic, snap the Obscurer into my belt, and head to the Portal—it's getting late.

Chapter Nineteen

The bungalow is quiet, but we're all restless.

"Maybe if we talk about it," Sage says, "we'll be able to get some sleep. You know, like process all that horrible stuff we saw."

"Yeah," Will agrees. "I'm worried about the shaman. He saw Grimshaw and knows what Chronnite's planning to do to the rainforest. A witness is far more powerful than our video footage. People might think the video was created with A.I."

"Oh, that's a terrible thought!" Sage groans. "There's got to be a way to prove it's real. I shouldn't have crushed the city model. That was hard evidence."

"It was way too big to carry out," Jack says.

"Jack, that's it!" I say. "What if Kayou is still inside Death Cavern?"

Will clears his throat. "We never saw any footage of him being carried out, that's for sure."

"I think we should go back and investigate,

see if he's locked in some backroom. Or at least look for clues to where they could've taken him."

"Yeah, he risked everything. We need to look for him." Sage agrees.

"The police have control of the building," Jack says. "It's a good idea, but not much chance of getting inside. And if Kayou's in there, the police probably found him by now."

"We can't trust the police! They weren't even willing to look for him, remember?"

"Let's talk about it tomorrow," Jack sighs, closing his eyes.

"Yeah," Will agrees.

I get it. They're afraid.

I close my eyes, but my mind won't settle. I keep seeing those men beating up Kayou and dragging him away.

Is he still alive?

I think about Kayou, and the future city, and my heart does weird stuff, racing and skipping beats all at once. Then, I think about the jaguar. I wonder how it's doing. Is it out of pain? How long will it be before it's healed? Before it returns to the rainforest?

How many jaguars have suffered and died in this horrible way? The tables filled with skulls, claws, and teeth haunt me. *How can people be so cruel?*

The strong, muscular body of the jaguar that welcomed us to Ecuador sprints across my mind.

Fierce beauty.

I flip back in time to the jaguar fundraiser, then to Norbu, and back to this afternoon—and the exact moment my eyes met the jaguar's. I try to re-experience the connection. And end up thinking of Zara. I clutch my locket tightly and call her eyes to mind.

Where are you? I miss you. I love you.

I take a deep breath, release it, and repeat, pretending that Sage is leading me in meditation. As I breathe, my focus moves from my breath to the eyes of the jaguar. Deeper and deeper, I go, into its eyes.

In the distance, I hear a low mournful note. Someone is playing the quena. The melody is familiar and calls me. I move through a dark forest toward the sound. The darkness shrouds everything in a blanket of obscurity, but the haunting melody continues. Each note pierces the silence, urging me to follow it deeper into the forest.

The melody grows loud and foreboding. My heart races. I look for Zara, but she's nowhere in sight. The darkness lifts and the forest morphs into a neon city. Cars honk and sirens wail, drowning out the melody of the quena.

A deep and terrible pain arises in my chest. I step back, faster and faster, until I'm running backward through the forest. I trip and fall.

A jaguar pounces from behind a tree, blocking my path, its fierce gaze fixed on mine—a low growl turns into a deafening roar.

I wake with Sage shaking me. "Come on, it's time for the dream-sharing ceremony."

I roll off the hammock and follow my friends to the gathering, where the community is already pouring the Wayusa tea. We sip the tea and take turns listening as the dreams are shared and the interpretations made.

"This is going to sound really weird," Will says, "but I dreamed of an eagle with strange feathers soaring over a field of glowing mushrooms. And a llama walking the slopes of the Andes." He rubs his forehead.

The elders make quite a lot of that dream and suggest Will has been visited by the Harpy Eagle, a powerful symbol of spirit. It is a favorable dream. Will says the dream reminded him of his home in Arkansas where he sees eagles, and of his family's mushroom farm, though he can't explain the glow.

"My dream," Jack starts, "was confusing, but I remember a bright purple frog—I think it was a poison dart frog, but I haven't seen one like it."

Sage has the most elaborate dream of all, with rare plants, a glowing pink dolphin, bright yellow orchids, a hummingbird, and even a sloth—which she's been longing to see. The elders' consensus is that Arutam is speaking through ever-changing forms.

When I share my jaguar dream, the elders suggest that the jaguar is preparing me for a time when I will once again be asked to "touch my fears."

That feels right.

I never thought these missions would be easy. I just knew I couldn't turn my back on the future.

When *Hora de Wayusa* is over, I suggest we take a walk.

"Wish I could go," Remi says, "but guests are arriving today. Don't get lost."

"No worries," I say with a grin. "We've got caiman fighters."

"Dude." Jack punches my arm and looks away, making me wonder if he has a crush on Remi.

Sorry, I mouth.

He glares as if to say, *It's not like that*. But I've known him nearly forever, and that was a new look.

"Okay, you've got my number," Remi calls. "I'll see you when you're ready to head to the city to pick up your van."

"Sounds great," I wave.

We walk down the wooden walkway and onto the forest path. We're nearing the riverbank when I turn to the others. "Let's take the canoes and return to the cavern to see if we can find the shaman or at least look for clues."

"No." Jack shakes his head. "I don't think that's a good idea. Last time Remi helped us navigate the river. Remember? She's a forest guardian—she doesn't live in the forest; she is the forest. You don't know anything about the rainforest."

Jack's words hit me like a slap in the face. He has never compared me to another person and made me come up short. I might not be a forest guardian, but I feel a kinship with the Dream People of the Amazon and I'm not about to give up on the shaman.

"You guys don't have to come," I snap. "Sage and I will go. If the police are there, we'll say we lost our phone. Once we're inside, we'll have a look around."

Will signals Jack. They huddle. "On second thought, we'll join you," Will says diplomatically.

"Seriously, we're good," I protest. I'm not looking forward to hearing Jack complain and worry for hours.

"Scoot over," Jack grumbles, stepping into the canoe. "I care about the shaman, too. I just hope we see river dolphins and not caiman."

Our paddles dip quietly into the water, rhythmically propelling the canoe forward; the morning mist clings to the water's surface like a billowy white veil. A symphony of hoots, whistles, and caws fills the air as the forest awakens, teeming with life.

"Look up there!" Sage points toward the canopy, where a flash of vibrant colors streaks across the sky. A pair of scarlet macaws, with their bright red and yellow feathers, soar above.

"My parents really need to come here," I say, snapping some pics.

"Yeah, I'd love to bring my mom," Sage says. "Hey, check out that huge ceiba tree," she adds, gesturing to a massive tree on the riverbank with an immense trunk.

Will points to some monkeys, their guttural calls echoing through the trees. "Wonder if they're arguing over breakfast," he jokes, lightening the mood.

We round a bend, and the river opens before us.

"Hey, look over there!" I say, motioning ahead. A pink river dophin surfaces gracefully, its skin glistens in the sunlight before it dives back into the depths. When it resurfaces, several more dolphin appear alongside.

"Yay!" Sage exclaims. We stop paddling to watch the playful pod.

"Check out the size of that one," Will says.

Sage leans forward. "Look, it's glowing—just like the dolphin in my dream! I can almost touch it!" She laughs, reaching into the water.

Her excitement is infectious. We all lean forward to see. The shift of our weight throws the canoe off balance, and it tilts sharply.

"Watch out!" Will shouts as we scramble to stabilize the canoe.

Sage and I lean to opposite sides, attempting to counterbalance the sudden shift, but our movements are hasty and panicked. The canoe overturns, plunging us into the river. Water closes over my head, a shock of cold that scrambles my senses. I kick toward the surface, gasping for air, my heart pounding in my ears.

One by one, heads emerge from the water, wide-eyed and spluttering.

"Grab the canoe!" I shout, swimming frantically to reach it.

"Let it go!" Will yells.

I don't want to give up, but I remember how quickly Will and Jack were carried away by the current, so I swim back to my friends.

"Great, just great!" Jack grumbles. "I knew something like this would happen!"

"Your negative thinking probably made it happen," Sage snaps.

"Come on, stop fighting, and let's get out of here before the piranhas get us," Will says. "Or a caiman starts looking for breakfast."

Jack gives me the stink eye.

We swim to the riverbank and collapse, panting heavily, our clothes clinging to our bodies.

"What are we going to do now, Lexa?" Jack fumes. "I'm sure Kapawi isn't going to thank us for losing a canoe."

"You worried Remi's going to be mad at you?" I half-taunt, half-tease.

"I wonder if she'll come looking for us?" Sage says.

"I hope not!" Jack groans. "We haven't gone far. I'm sure we can walk back before dark."

Jack has a crush on Remi. I wasn't sure before, but now I'm certain. I fight the urge to say something snarky.

"The upside," Sage says, "is we're back on dry land and no one is injured."

"Yeah," I reply, trying to hide my disappointment. Without the canoe, there's no way we can find our way back to Death Cavern. No way to search for the shaman, or clues to his disappearance. The village is too far away. I reach for my phone to map our location.

"My phone! I've lost it!" I shout.

"Are you sure?" Jack asks, worriedly.

I throw my hands out. "Yes!"

"Must be at the bottom of the river by now," Sage says matter-of-factly.

Jack shakes his head. "Great. Just great. Now we have no way to communicate. This is what happens when you go off unprepared."

WIll sighs and rubs his forehead.

"Oh my gosh!" Sage exclaims. "Look, over there."

She points into the forest. "It's a sloth! I can't believe it!"

She's giddy with excitement. "It must be pooping," she adds. "That's one of the things they do when they come down from the trees. Come on, let's go."

Jack frowns. "Wait. Did she just say the sloth is pooping?"

"Gross!" Will grimaces.

I palm my face. "We'll catch up," I call as Sage sprints into the forest.

The boys lie back on the shore, drying their clothes in the morning sun.

"I'm going to look for my phone," I say, heading for the riverbank. The implications of losing my phone tumbling through my head like dominoes.

What if my data didn't back up to the cloud last night?

Have I lost the footage of Kayou?

Of Chronnite's plan to build a city in the rainforest?

I take a deep breath and exhale slowly, trying to calm the rising panic. I force myself to focus on my surroundings.

A bright green lizard catches my eye. It scurries off and I follow it to the roots of a vast kapok, where I spot a few bright red feathers. Could they be from a scarlet macaw? I put the feathers in my pocket, deciding to gift them to my parents later.

I hear the boys calling my name and head back.

"Ouch," I say, slapping my arms. "I'm under an invisible bug attack."

"Yeah, me, too," Jack grumbles. "I don't see anything, do you?"

"Must be some kind of Amazonian no-see-ums," Will suggests.

"Let's go check out the sloth. It's probably moved a couple of inches—the poop might have fallen out of its butt," I joke, trying to take my mind off my lost phone.

"Lexa, you're gross," Will says.

The boys laugh. We slap at invisible bugs on our arms and legs, and head toward the trees.

"Sage," I call as we enter the canopy.

She doesn't reply.

I look at the boys. "Which way did she go?"

They shrug.

"I thought you were watching," Will says.

I shake my head.

"She can't be far," Jack says.

"Sage," I call again.

"Saaaage . . ." Will shouts, putting more force behind it.

My heart pounds as we push further through the underbrush.

After several more attempts, Jack says, "We need a plan. We can't just wander aimlessly around or we'll get lost."

I nod in agreement, grateful Jack sounds like his usual self again. We're in a dangerous situation, and we need to think clearly if we're going to find Sage.

"Okay," Jack says, "Let's stick together and keep track of where we've searched so we don't end up going in circles.

"We'll search the surrounding area first and stay within shouting distance of each other. We can mark the places we've searched, so we don't go over them again.

"Here," Jack pulls a bag of snap noise-makers from his pocket. "These probably won't work anymore, might as well use them."

I expect him to glare at me, but he doesn't. The only thing I see in his eyes is concern.

"We'll find her, Lex. We have to."

His words unlock a memory. A wave of panic washes over me.

Jack said the same thing the night Zara disappeared.

I place my hand on my chest, trying to calm the rapid thumping of my heart. The sound echoes in my ears, drowning out all other noises.

Chapter Twenty

The Agency goes dark at night to encourage stargazing and constellation bathing—the source of many Inspirations, including the Quantum Globe. I'm grateful for the darkness as I slip out of my room and into the corridor, making my way to the Hall of Mirrors, lit by only the dimness of candlelight.

The plans in my head aren't as clear as I'd like. In the past, I've calculated each location with precision. But tonight, no amount of planning can prepare me for the unpredictable nature of what I'm about to do. Fortunately, the Portal's security is a joke—no cameras or motion sensors, just a rotation of Masters who consider it an honor to stroll around in the evenings. They don't expect anyone to break the rules because rule-breakers don't last at the Agency. And if you've made it into the Agency, you worked hard to get here or had a stroke of good fortune, like me, to be orphaned inside.

That's all I know about my origins. *Inside* the Agency has only recently piqued my curiosity. Pasha says I was found in my room and have always lived there. That feels right because I don't remember anything else.

Midnight.

There is a pattern and rhythm to the nightly patrols, which I have learned well.

Shift change is the weakest link in Portal protection because the Masters can't pass up an opportunity to talk. All I need is a sliver of a chance to dash through the Portal.

Tonight, Master Fontane will be patrolling and handing off to Masayuki. Fontane and Masayuki don't speak much, so this hand-off combination makes things more challenging.

I run my fingers over the cold stone of the Quantum Obscurer for reassurance. My heart hammers against my ribs as I move closer to the Portal's entrance. I know what awaits me—danger, uncertainty, maybe even a one-way trip to oblivion. But I can't let everyone down, not when so much is at stake. I must go back into the past to create a new future—or at least hold open the possibilities. That's what I always tell myself. It makes breaking the rules easier.

I take a deep breath, filling my lungs and steadying my nerves. Glancing toward Masayuki and Fontane, I step out of the shadows, feeling the familiar tug at the edge of my reality. I'm stepping toward the Portal when I hear my name.

"Is that you, Norbu?" Masayuki calls out.

My heart skips a beat. I step back, cover the Obscurer, and try to think of my next move.

"Yes, Masayuki," I say, moving toward him to put distance between myself and the Portal.

"What are you doing here? It's late," he says in a disapproving tone.

"I'm . . . I'm looking for Radhika."

"Radhika?" Masayuki repeats, questioningly.

I regret mentioning her name, but I nod anyway.

Masayuki glances around as if Radhika might walk by, which we both know is highly unlikely. He doesn't accuse me of lying but speaks solemnly, "Norbu, go to your room and stay there until I call for you. Do you understand?"

I feel a lump in my throat and lower my gaze, ashamed and embarrassed, wishing I could disappear and never face him again.

Without looking up, I turn and move silently through the passages into the corridors, through the Hall of Shame, where I see Pasha.

"What happened?" she whisper-purrs. "Did he catch you?"

"No, but he ordered me to stay in my room. I'm going to be kicked out and the possible future I was trying to create is collapsing or already has."

"You need to find out, hurry, go use the quantum globe."

"I don't want to look."

"Maybe you can do something . . . You always say that it's because people blind their eyes and hearts to the pain of their world that they don't do anything to stop it. You're doing that now."

I pick up my pace and slip into my room, pulling the curtain across my door to prevent the light from escaping—the mini quantum globe glows more brightly at night when the Agency has gone dark.

"Do you think he knows?"

"He suspects, but if he knew, you would be out." Pasha doesn't mince words. "Perhaps he simply plans to give you a warning. Right now, you don't have time to think about that. You need to think about the team, the shaman, the future you've set in motion."

"Yeah, right." I sigh, taking the Obscurer out of my belt. "I was seconds away from activating it. The blue spark would have given me away. Timing is everything."

"Then stop wasting it!" Pasha hisses.

I take the quantum globe off the shelf and sit on my cushion. Do I really want to know, or would it be better to stop looking?

"They who hesitate are lost!" Pasha reprimands. "Go on, activate it."

I place my finger on the stone, roll it three times, and watch the orb of light expand.

"Well? What do you see? Has it broken? Is there still time?"

"Pasha . . . please, I need to concentrate."

"Well?" Pasha complains.

"Things are . . . moving . . . altering . . ."

"For better or ?"

"For worse . . . there's notable Unraveling."

"Get in there and do something," Pasha hisses.

"What can I do? You know Lexa can't communicate through dream travel."

"But the shaman can," Pasha reminds. "See what's happening to him. Maybe you can help."

I pick her up and gaze into her soft, sky-blue eyes. "I love you."

"Me too," she purrs.

I place her on the sofa, light my favorite incense, the Seifui blend of sandalwood, clove, and cinnamon, and sit. There's no time for extended preparations. My previous practice must benefit me now. I close my eyes and breathe. In breath, out breath, right nostril, left nostril, clearing energy channels throughout my body. Settling. Focusing. Deepening until my mind opens to the quantum field of all possibilities, where I hold the Intention to find the shaman. When I do, I feel great pain and sorrow. Kayou's hands are still bound, and he has little food or water for days. The guard stares at his phone, occasionally sipping from a bottle. Kayou isn't chanting but is wide awake.

"Norbu," he greets. "Lexa and her friends are lost in the forest, but nearby. We must see to their safety."

"How can I help?"

"Enter the Circle, hold the Intention," he replies.

The shaman opens his field of consciousness. Inside, I become one of a thousand shimmering butterflies feeding on sweet nectar. I am the whole rainforest. Everything is alive and glowing, the colors are hyper-intense, and all sounds are harmonious.

A large white butterfly flies in, circles around his head, and flies out. A small green lizard scurries across the dirt floor, climbs up the wall, and out the window. Outside the window, a hummingbird hovers. A tiny, purple frog sits on the windowsill, next to a hollow reed.

Chapter Twenty-One

We search every inch of the nearby forest for Sage, but as the hours tick by, hope dwindles, and exhaustion sets in.

"How could she wander so far away?" I say. "I don't get it."

Will lets out a worried sigh. "What if something bad happened to her?"

Jack grimaces. "Like a jaguar..."

"Shh! Don't say it!" I shout. "You know how Sage thinks, you'll bring it on her!"

"Sorry." Jack winces. "She must be getting scared, out here all alone."

We're feeling anxious, and the weight of our guilt is increasingly heavy. Why were we lolling around on the shore anyway? Why didn't we go with her? Seeing a sloth was far more interesting than anything we were doing.

I'm filled with regret, anxiety, and guilt. I had promised Ms. Paterson I'd look after her daughter, and now I've gone and lost her. I should have planned the return to the cavern instead of taking off unprepared. Jack's right. This is Remi's home. I should have asked her to lead us back to the cavern. My impatience and arrogance have caused us to lose Sage.

In the midst of my gloom, a strange iridescent glimmer catches the corner of my eye. I look up as a large white butterfly soars into the canopy. And it hits me.

"Sloths hang from the trees! Sage must be in the canopy!" I shout, my heart pounding with excitement. I run into the forest, calling her name into the trees.

"Lexa! Stop, you're going the wrong way," Jack yells. "There's no snaps in that direction." Jack waves his hands in the air in exasperation. "If she's in the canopy, we need to return to where we entered the forest and start the search over. Can you and Will stay put for like five minutes?"

Jack looks around, moving a hundred yards out and back in all directions, and returns, discouraged. "The foliage is so thick," he says. "I guess snaps were a bad idea."

Frustratedly, he kicks the underbrush; a tiny, vibrant purple frog jumps out.

"Woah! Dude," Will says. "Look at those colors!"

The bright violet frog hops toward Jack. He crouches to get a closer look. "Wow. It's a harlequin frog. Check out these patterns."

We gather around.

"That's a poison dart frog," Will says.

"Nah, look at the way the pattern moves across the mid—" Jack pauses suddenly, adjusts his glasses, and grins. "I see a snap!" He leaps up.

"A snap!" we yell together. We're back on the path.

We move forward more cautiously. Jack keeps his eyes on the underbrush for snaps, and Will and I call into the trees.

"Sage," I yell, my throat hoarse from the effort.

"I'm up here," her voice drifts down from the canopy.

We run toward the sound, hearts racing.

"Where are you?" Jack calls.

"Up here!" Sage yells. She's perched casually in a tree and looks at us with big innocent eyes.

"Sage!" I exclaim, relief flooding my body. "Thank goodness you're okay!"

"What?" she says. "Why wouldn't I be?"

"We've been searching for you for hours," I reply.

Her expression swiftly morphs. "Oh! I didn't realize—I was just . . ." She falters, gesturing toward a cluster of bright yellow flowers.

"Coming down," she says sheepishly, her eyes still fixed on the flowers as she jumps to the ground.

We gather around her, a mix of relief and annoyance washing over us.

"What were you thinking?" I scold.

"I just wanted to take a closer look," Sage says defensively, holding the flower out for us to see. "It's an orchid, and it smells amazing!"

"You could have been lost," Jack says. "Do you even realize that? We're supposed to stay together."

"I'm sorry," Sage apologizes, finally tearing her gaze away from the flower to meet our worried faces. "I guess I lost track of time."

"That's for sure," Will says. "Glad you're okay."

Sage winces. "Thanks. Now let me show you what I've collected!" She moves to the base of a nearby tree. Under it is a newly woven basket laden with plants. "Meena taught me about these plants, and they are really useful. Some of them are quite rare. I'm taking them back to the tribe. Is it time to leave *already*?"

Jack shakes his head. "When you were weaving that basket, did you even think about us once?"

"Ugh," she groans. "I said I'm sorry!"

Will looks around the area. "Do you think we should camp here?" he asks. "Build a shelter before dark?"

"Wait, is it really *that* late?" Sage asks.

We stare at her.

She shrugs. "We can always climb up the trees to avoid the predators. That's why the sloths live up there. It's safer. Some of them live for like thirty years so we have a good chance of survival."

"Sage, sometimes you put your foot in your mouth," Jack says.

"Jack, sometimes you fart," she says back.

"Guys!" Will says. "This is serious. It takes time to set up a campsite." Suddenly, he grabs his ankle; his face contorting in pain. "Something bit me," he gasps.

"What was it? Did you see it? I hope it wasn't a *Fer de Lance*," Sage says, her voice trailing off.

"You just did it again," Jack says.

Will clutches his ankle.

"Show me," Sage demands, her voice steady despite the rising panic. We huddle around Will and see two puncture marks on his skin.

"Stay calm, Will," Sage says. "I have the plant for this in my basket."

I fight the urge to scream. Instead, I watch Sage sort through her basket.

"Here it is!" She holds up a plant, "This can slow the venom."

Sage strips a few leaves off the plant and then chews the leaves and applies the macerated pulp to Will's wound.

"Thank you, Sage," Will murmurs after a moment, the pain in his voice lessening.

"If it's not deadly venom, then you'll be okay," she says. "We'll know shortly."

Jack shakes his head.

"I don't mean it like that." Sage glares. "It's just the facts."

We huddle around Will in tense silence while we wait. He is sweating profusely, and his breathing is shallow. Sage sits by his side, her hand resting on his shoulder, comfortingly.

"Where's your asthma inhaler?" I ask.

"Back in the bungalow." Will shrugs. "I didn't think I'd need it this morning."

My heart pounds. "I'm so sorry, Will," I say, "I didn't mean to . . ."

"Lexa, it's not your fault that a snake bit me, don't even start blaming yourself."

I look around and notice the changing light; it's getting late. We have no shelter or food, and now Will is injured.

"We need to start a fire," I say, breaking the heavy silence that hangs over us.

"We don't have our bags, so no matches or lighters," Jack points out. "I could kick myself for going on this walk without my bag."

I had tried to make Jack stay behind, but I still feel guilty. He would have never set out on a hike to Death Cavern unprepared if he hadn't felt pressured.

"Maybe we could do it the old-fashioned way," I say, "gather up some dry leaves and sticks and—"

Jack cuts me off, "Lexa, the wearable... it's glowing."

I look down to see an orange glow.

"Is she coming to help us?" Sage asks, hopefully.

"I haven't been thinking of her," I admit. "But maybe..."

The wearable stops blinking but Zara's nowhere in sight.

"I guess it was a false alarm," I say.

"A glitch in the quantum field," Will muses, a faint smile on his face. The pain has let up. "Looks like I am going to survive." He grins.

A soft, ethereal sound delicately tickles my ear. It floats on the breeze, almost imperceptible yet hauntingly beautiful. "Do you guys hear that?"

"What?" Jack asks.

"The sounds of the quena."

Chapter Twenty-Two

Half in, half out, on the window's ledge, the wind moves through the hollow reed, and the melody rises and falls.

Everything unfolds. I focus on the Intention, even when the wearable glows. Worrying about the quantum actuator or the future won't help anything now. Being fully present where I am is all that matters.

"This way," Lexa says, clearly hearing the melody the shaman plays.

"What?" Jack shakes his head. "I don't hear anything." He looks to Will and Sage. "Do you?"

They shake their heads in bewilderment.

"I heard it again, come on. Maybe we're near a village."

"Oh my gosh!" Sage exclaims. "Look! Over there, that's the most beautiful hummingbird I've ever seen!" She chases the hummingbird as it flits through the air.

"Shhh," Lexa frets, "I can't hear the tune."

Sage shrugs. "Maybe it was the buzz of the hummingbird." She runs ahead; they chase, unwilling to let Sage slip out of sight.

The hummingbird leads Sage north a few feet, then westward, stopping to hover low, a hundred feet in front of the hidden prison. She sees the guard, turns around and frantically throws her arms out to her sides, signaling the team to stop and blocking forward passage. She brings one finger to her lips, gesturing for silence.

The others pick up on her distress and creep cautiously forward through the foliage where she's crouched.

"Look," she whispers.

The guard, now snoring in a stupor, is seated in front of the hidden jail with its tiny, barred window.

As they stare, a Saluki appears. She isn't blue but an ethereal white.

"Zara?" Lexa whispers. "Wait." She shakes her head and turns to her friends. "Are you guys seeing what I'm seeing?"

They nod, eyes wide. Lexa looks down at her wearable; they follow her gaze. It's not glowing.

Their eyes travel back to Zara. She morphs into a jaguar. The shift is reminiscent of a dreamscape.

"Did you see that?" Lexa asks.

They nod, mystified.

"Is Zara doing that?" Sage asks.

"I don't think so," Lexa admits.

"Is Norbu?" Will asks.

"No." Lexa shakes her head. "I've seen this before," she says, "in a dream." She closes her eyes and searches for answers. In her dreamscape, she hears a far-off melody. The realization comes at once. "The shaman is doing this. Kayou's in there," she whispers.

"You're sure about that?" Jack asks.

Lexa nods, enthusiastically. "Yes, we've got to get him out."

Her confidence is contagious.

"We need a plan," Jack says.

"We need to disable the guard," Will adds.

I've got toxic fibers," Sage says. "If we can get it in his mouth, it will poison him—temporarily."

"You planning to sneak up and put it in his mouth?" Jack whispers.

She glares at him. "Of course. I'm much quieter than any of you."

Lexa shakes her head. "That's too risky." She rubs her temples. "There has to be another way."

"Blow guns?" Will suggests.

Lexa nods.

Sage eyes her basket. "I'll make the poison. It won't be the same poison the Achuar use because we'd need to boil the plant and, well, I don't know all the preparations. But this"—she points to a plant in her basket—"should keep him asleep."

Lexa remembers the feathers she collected while following the lizard under the ceiba tree and removes a red feather from her pocket. "I'll make the darts."

"They need to be tiny," Sage says. "I'll show you."

Will turns to Jack. "Let's find some wood."

The Achuar have taught them well. They work quickly and quietly.

"Okay," Sage says. "Remember, these darts are toxic. Handle carefully."

One by one, they place the makeshift blowguns in their mouths and blow—tiny darts fly. Many misses, but one hit. The guard slaps his face, as if swatting a bug away.

They wait; his snore deepens. They slip quietly through the forest and crouch beside the window, peering in.

"Kayou," Lexa whispers. "Is that you?"

"Yes," he whispers in return.

The guard snores, slumped and half-dangling off the side of the chair.

"We're going to get you out of here."

Sage sneaks around to the guard.

Night falls.

She lifts the key.

Moments stretch.

The door opens.

The shaman steps into the forest he never left. Owls hoot, insects buzz, and fireflies flit. The shaman leads them to the safety of his village and teaches them the Achuar words for glow worms, railroad worms, and bioluminescent fungi.

In the Circle, I see a harpy eagle flying above a trail of bioluminescence beneath a canopy of stars. As I take in the beauty, I hear a faint whisper calling out my name. It sounds like it's coming from a far-off tunnel, echoing through the distance.

It's not Kayou's voice, but Pasha's.

"Come back now!" she hisses, distressed.

I open my eyes.

Masayuki stands in my room.

Chapter Twenty-Three

Word of the shaman's return spreads quickly, and soon Shakai, Remi, Taish, Taku, Meena, and many other Achuar people come to Kayou's village to celebrate. The quena fills the air and we feast like we haven't seen food in a week. When everyone is finished, we gather around the fire.

"I got wind of the meeting, disguised myself, and slipped in," Kayou says. "That's when I learned about the so-called City of the Future. Have you ever heard the saying, 'Inch by inch, it's a cinch. Yard by yard, it's very hard?'"

"Yes." I nod. "My parents love old sayings like that."

"So does Grimshaw. He buys up small plots of land by sending in people who seem to be all about protecting the rainforest, even some well-meaning nonprofits, but when one looks closely, they all lead back to Chronnite."

"That explains why Mr. Milnex was at the meeting," Jack says.

Remi frowns at Jack. "How come you know

someone who was at that meeting?"

"Mr. Milnex works at EverSave, where our parents work," Jack explains.

"Wait! Your parents work with the guy at the meeting?" Remi asks, horrified.

Jack's face goes red. "EverSave's not involved. It's a long story," he mumbles.

Remi looks around the circle. "We've got time, don't we, guys?"

Everyone nods.

"Uh . . ." Jack begins. "We were at Thistleton Academy, a green school for creative types"—he looks at the rest of us for support—"when we discovered Chronnite had taken over the school."

Jack is mortified. I'm not eager to explain things, but I don't have a crush on Remi, so I step up.

"The school wasn't like it was supposed to be," I say. "We started investigating and found footage of Thistleton's graduates working with companies owned by Chronnite. We saw the EverSave logo on some people who looked like they were involved in suspicious activities."

"Yeah." Remi frowns. "I've seen the logo."

My face feels hot. I feel protective of our parents and great-aunt Beatrice.

Will notices, and takes over. "Lexa's dad

discovered that Mr. Milnex added a clause to EverSave's founding charter, giving it the right to serve as an ombudsman to oversee corporate activities. Chronnite was behind all of it.

"Yeah," Sage adds. "And our parents are suing Thistleton, trying to prove that Chronnite broke the original contract requiring them to keep the school's fouding mission intact. Now they are selling their status-quo lesson plans to schools all over the world."

Kayou clears his throat. "What our guests have done is heroic. Education is the heart of a culture. Did you ever wonder why a corporation as big as Chronnite would be involved in the illegal trade of jaguars?"

Will speaks up, "We figured it was because they are part of a criminal syndicate."

Kayou nods. "That's a good guess. Chronnite participates in criminal activities, but most criminal syndicates are after the money. Grimshaw makes plenty of money from legal businesses. He supports the trade in jaguar parts because he seeks to kill our culture. He can't buy up the rainforest if we're unwilling to sell it. But if he can kill our culture—our connection to the rainforest—our spirit, he has a way in."

"Shakai taught us that the jaguar means

touching your fears," I say, grappling to understand. "Are you saying Grimshaw is killing off jaguars to make people afraid?"

Kayou nods solemnly.

"Grimshaw has studied history. He knows that the best way to take over the land is to break the spirit of the people. Spirit is part of a culture and is transmitted through how we live and what we teach our children. By killing off the jaguars, Grimshaw aims to make us afraid, to keep us from speaking up, protesting, and fighting back."

"But Remi and her friends aren't going to let that happen," Jack says, catching Remi's eye.

"Not if they remember they are part of the Prophecy," Kayou says. "As are we all."

"Wait, us too? We're part of a prophecy? Sage asks, eyes wide.

Kayou nods. "The *Prophecy of the Eagle and the Condor* arose from the dreams of our ancestors, visionaries who could see future possibilities. They foresaw a time marked by the separation of the head and heart.

"The Eagle represented the head, or intellect, and symbolized control over the physical world," Kayou explains. "This path led to technological advancements, towering skyscrapers, and a globally connected yet fragmented society where progress often overshadows the human spirit.

"The Condor symbolized the heart. This path meandered through the deep forests where the pulse of Pachamama beats strongest, where wisdom is found in the living web of existence.

"The prophecy foretold a time when the Eagle and the Condor would fly separately, representing a divided world. However, it also foretold that a time would arrive when the spirits of the Eagle and the Condor would merge in a dance of renewal.

"This era is called *Pachakuti* and marks the beginning of a new age in which the strengths of the mind would serve the wisdom of the heart, and the technological advancements of the Eagle would exist in harmony with the ecological balance cherished by the Condor."

He pauses.

"Now, I will share an important truth that powerful forces are actively trying to keep from you."

We lean in.

"You, and you, and you"—he looks to each of us—"are living during this time, the time of Pachakuti, or the Great Turning.

"By awakening both sides of your nature—mind and heart—you can create a future where every action and choice is made with the understanding of our interconnectedness. When doubts arise, remind yourselves that you are alive at a crucial time in history.

"Repeat with me: I am alive at a crucial time in history. Together we can create a harmonious world where all beings can thrive in the sacred dance of existence."

We repeat the shaman's words.

"Will you tell us more about the prophecy?" Sage asks.

"Tomorrow," Kayou replies, gently. "It is late, and we have all had a long day."

Sage grumbles. Then, remembering that Kayou has been a prisoner, says, "Of course, you must be exhausted."

Kayou smiles.

Jack doesn't give Sage the stink eye, or if he does, I miss it.

As I lie down to sleep, every muscle and bone in my body feels heavy. Even my ordinarily overactive mind is tired. There's only one thought swirling at the edges—what Kayou said about us living in a crucial time reminds me of something Norbu said. He didn't use the word *Pachakuti*, but maybe the great turning? I need to ask the others if they remember.

Could Norbu know Kayou?

Does that even make sense?

No. I'm just overly tired.

Just before I nod off, I replay the moment when we found the prison. The moment Zara appeared.

How did you do that? Thank you. I love you.

Chapter Twenty-Four

"I am aware of certain activities," Masayuki begins. "Do you have anything to say for yourself?"

My heart pounds as I stand before him, avoiding eye contact and feeling the weight of his disappointment.

"I . . ." I stutter, struggling to find words. "I was trying to . . ."

"You put yourself above the rules and endangered everyone," Masayuki interrupts.

"I'm sorry," I whisper, as tears fall.

Pasha climbs onto my shoulder and nuzzles my neck.

Masayuki sighs heavily. "Prepare yourself and meet us in the Great Round," he instructs before leaving the room.

My vision blurs as more tears fill my eyes. My heart races as I struggle to compose myself. I can't bring myself to face the Masters, not after what I've done. They won't just scold me; expulsion is the least I can expect.

"Norbu?" Pasha's voice is soft, but I can't look at her. I lift her from my shoulder and place her on her favorite pillow.

I gather my belongings and shove them into my bag.

Pasha pounces. "You can't just run away. You're scared, but you don't have to face them alone. I'll go with you."

"Stay out of this," I mutter, avoiding her luminous eyes. "Remember our deal. You had no part of this."

"Then I'll run away with you," she declares.

"No. That's not possible." My response is sharper than intended. "It's not safe for you out there."

"Would you really leave me?" she asks, her voice trembling.

"Pasha, I have nothing out there. No family, no friends, no plan, no place to go. It's no life for you."

She flinches, hurt by my words.

"I promise this is for the best."

She turns away, her small frame shaking.

Her suffering cuts deeper than any reprimand from Masayuki. Guilt tightens its grip around my heart, but it can't be helped. Pasha will have food, water, and shelter here—none of which I can promise her outside. She doesn't understand that I'm trying to protect her.

I sling my bag over my shoulder and slip out without looking back. I'm thankful I won't pass through the Hall of Mirrors on my way out of the building.

Outside, the air is cool, and the moon hangs low and full, casting a pale light over the mountain landscape. Its silent presence follows me as I walk down a narrow path that leads into the valley. Each step takes me further away from everything I've ever known—the Agency, Pasha, and my hopes for a life as an Agent. I'm leaving behind access to the Portal—and with it, my only way to communicate with my friends in the past. Sure, I'll be able to dream-travel and witness some of what takes place, but I won't be able to speak to anyone—or to help. I'll be just another voyeur in time.

What will they think of me when I never show up again?

My heart aches with deep pain. A vast hollowness fills me, as if nothing has any meaning. A heaviness on my soul. *Hopelessness.* As I experience this emotion for the first time, I feel a strong empathy for those who have felt it before. I have been so fortunate to have never known this pain until now.

I have had Pasha, the Agency, and my friends, for as long as I can remember. Gratitude fills my heart—how fortunate I was! Tears of gratitude join those of sorrow, and suddenly, a great orb of luminescence glows before me.

"Norbu," a voice calls out, resonating from the heart of the light. It's neither male nor female, but it knows my name—it must be a quantum-field hologram, one of G.A.I.A.'s more advanced methods of communication that I've never experienced.

"Return to the Agency." The command is firm yet oddly soothing. I squint against the brightness, trying to discern the source, but there's only the pulsating light. "You have a place within the balance," the voice intones.

In the intense presence of the light, it is impossible to ignore my responsibilities and the consequences of my choices.

I shut my eyes tightly, trying to escape the light. But I know the truth. My actions will catch up with me no matter how far I flee. The ties between cause and effect will hold me accountable.

I decide to return to the Agency and, as I do, the bright sphere of light breaks into numerous smaller orbs . . . an ethereal murmuration, leading me to face the consequences of my actions.

Chapter Twenty-Five

It's time to leave Kapawi, but we're dragging our feet. We're at loose ends with no instructions from the wearable, no sign of Zara, and no word from Norbu.

Finding Anatola is at the top of our list, so Will and Jack are narrowing down potential locations. Sage sits nearby, drawing an orchid. Jack glances over her shoulder.

"Why do you keep doing that?" he asks.

"What?" Sage frowns.

"Erasing everything you draw?"

"This is a botanical specimen. It needs to be perfect," she says, erasing the flower yet again.

"Hello," a voice calls from outside.

It's Kayou. We scramble to our feet.

"Do you have time for a walk?" he asks, peering inside the bungalow. "There's something I want to share with you."

We nod and eagerly follow Kayou out of the bungalow and into the forest. Before long, we stop at the base of a giant Brazil nut tree.

He points to the ground, where a dark brown rodent scurries by.

"We've seen lots of those," Jack says without mentioning how much he dislikes them.

"Agoutis have razor-sharp teeth," Kayou says. "They are the only creatures in the rainforest that can crack the hard pod of the Brazil nut. They hide seeds beneath the soil, dig them up, and rebury them again and again."

"Like squirrels?" Sage asks.

"Yes." Kayou nods. "Without agoutis to

spread its seeds, the Brazil nut tree would be doomed." He points to a bee buzzing around a nearby tree—not the Brazil nut, but another, shorter tree. "Do you see that bee?"

We nod.

"That is the large-bodied orchid bee. It's the only bee that pollinates the Brazil nut tree.

Many people say that the survival of the Brazil nut tree depends upon the agoutis and the bees. And it does, but if you look closer, there's much more."

We follow Kayou to the base of the shorter tree, where a large cluster of green orchids bloom.

"The bees can only reach the Brazil nut flowers at the top of the tree if the shorter, understory trees, like this one, are present."

Sage frowns. "Why?"

Kayou grins. "Orchid bees are somewhat lazy. If there aren't trees of various heights around, they tend to stick to flowers that are easy to reach—they'd never bother to fly high enough to reach the Brazil nut flowers if they didn't have a way to rest."

Kayou picks an orchid blossom and hands it to Sage. "And it would be unwise to overlook the role of the orchids."

Sage's face lights up. "Are orchids equally important?"

Kayou nods. "The male orchid bees perfume themselves with wild orchids to attract mates. So, without the orchids, the bees wouldn't reproduce. To preserve Brazil nut trees, we must preserve not only agoutis and orchid bees but smaller trees and orchids, too. The rainforest is a living system.

"I'm telling you this because I want you to recognize yourselves as part of the same living system. You may live far from the rainforest, like the orchid bee is far from the flowers, but you are vital to the rainforest's survival. Everyone has a role to play."

"People think I hate cities. It isn't that I hate cities. It's that I love rainforests. We need both; cities just need to be redesigned in keeping with principles of biomimicry."

"What's that?" Jack asks, frowning.

"Biomimicry is about learning from nature's designs and applying those principles to human innovation," Kayou explains, guiding us back to our bungalow. "For example, we can design water collection systems inspired by how bromeliad plants capture and store rainwater in their leaves. Solutions are plentiful; we just need to demand them.

"We need to shift the dream of the modern world from a culture of overconsumption to one that honors and sustains life."

I repeat Kayou's words silently, committing them to memory. I am a dreamer, like the Achuar people. I don't understand my dreams as well as they understand theirs, and I don't know how one goes about changing the dream of the modern world, but I'm willing to learn. And I know my friends are too.

We return to our bungalow and find Remi waiting for us. "Hey guys," she says. "Are you ready to head out?"

"We still have a few things to pack up," I say.

"Perfect." She smiles. "I've got a group of visitors to welcome; see you in an hour."

We nod. And then it's time to say goodbye to Kayou, which is harder than any of us imagined. There's something special about the shaman. Like he knows more about us than we know about ourselves.

"Keep up the work you are doing," Kayou says. "What you revealed at Thistleton is more important than you realize. And coming to investigate the jaguars and finding me took courage. You carry the jaguar spirit inside. Call upon it as you continue your journey. Grimshaw will stop at nothing to expand his corporate empire. He has invested Chronnite in outdated ways and is too greedy to change. He will come after what you love most to try to stop you."

A shiver runs down my spine. Sage's face goes pale. Will kicks the dirt. Jack takes off his glasses and rubs his eyes. None of us say anything, but we don't have to.

"You are not alone. Unseen, yet strong forces are aiding you." Kayou says, before waving goodbye and heading back to the forest.

We step inside the bungalow, and Jack says what I'm thinking, "Do you guys think there's any chance Kayou could know Norbu?"

"I was just thinking that."

"Me, too," Will says.

Sage clears her throat. "He might have been talking more generally, like about Arutam."

"True," I say.

Will looks thoughtful "Guys, I just realized I haven't needed my inhaler since the snake bit me. Isn't that strange?"

Sage shrugs. "No, not really. I think it makes sense. The venom might be the cure for whatever kind of asthma you have. Western science doesn't know about a lot of the medicine in the rainforest."

"Sage, that's impressive," Will says. "I sure wish I knew what kind of snake it was."

Sage tilts her head, deep in thought. "Or, it could be the combination of the venom and the plant medicine. Like Kayou said, everything works together."

"Could it be that you touched a fear or something like that?" I ask. "My therapist says that physical illnesses can be connected to our emotions. And, come to think about it, I haven't had an anxiety attack since we set foot in the rainforest. She'd probably say it's because I'm actively doing something to protect the environment."

"Yeah, that's right," Sage says. "The mind is powerful."

As we move to finish packing, she picks up her drawing from earlier and looks at it. "Hey, my orchid has been missing something," she says, smiling, "and I just figured out what it is."

She sketches a bee.

"The large-bodied orchid bee," Jack says, looking over her shoulder.

"Yep." She grins, filling in some details.

"That looks great," Jack says, but Sage is already erasing the bee.

"Oh no!" she groans. "It's ruined."

"Why?" Jack shakes his head, bewildered.

Sage holds up the paper. "I've erased so much I made a hole in it. I need better quality paper."

Jack stares at the paper, his eyes growing wide as a thought strikes. "Wait . . . That's it!" he shouts, turning to Will.

"Where's Anatola's journal?"

"Dude, slow down," Will says, though he hands over the journal over.

"Where's the rest of her stuff?" Jack demands. "The stuff she left under her bed in the dorm?"

Sage frowns. "Her toiletry bag?"

"Yes—do you have it?"

"Course I do; what do you need that for?"

Jack throws his hand up, frantically gesturing for her to get the bag.

By now, he has everyone's attention.

When Sage returns, he snatches the small cloth bag and dumps its contents on the floor. He passes his hand over the items like he's about to pull a rabbit from a hat, hovering over the lip gloss, before stopping on what looks like a tube of mascara.

"Ah ha! Here it is!" He picks up the mascara and waves it in the air. He turns the tube and pulls—instead of a wand, there's a marker. With one swift move, he opens the notebook and swipes the pen over the surface, erasing the top layer.

Will palms his face, but he doesn't try to stop Jack.

After a few strokes, words appear:

READ SILENTLY!!!!
Turn off ALL devices.
Do not hesitate or doubt.
Go to the hideout—one of you knows.
Do not share with B.E.L.A.
Disguise the van.
Do not use autopilot.
Do NOT fly!

We look up from the journal, taken aback.

Anatola knows about us!

Jack swipes his finger under the word "HIDEOUT" then draws a question mark.

Will turns the page and points to a sketch of a cave entrance, captioned *Time Warp Hollow*, then touches his chest.

We spontaneously hold hands, each thinking some version of the same thing:

Anatola went to great lengths to hide this message in a way that only we would find it.
We're in danger.
She knows more about the danger than we do.

We stand together, letting the truth sink in.

We aren't just kids on a series of critical missions.

We are part of something mysterious—part of Time itself.

We are yesterday.
We are today.
And tomorrow . . . knows our names.

With each thought, my resolve hardens. We are the carriers of hope in a place where greed seeks to overshadow the sacred.

We will not be deterred.

If you feel inspired to take action, consider starting an Environmental Club at your school.

Visit **MISSIONGAIA.COM** or scan the QR code to download free information and resources to help you get started.

AUTHOR'S NOTE

Many people, organizations, and companies around the world are working hard to address the challenges presented in this story. The good news is that there are far too many to list. If you'd like to learn more, here are some of those that inspired me while writing this book.

Pachamama Alliance:
https://pachamama.org/about

Kapawi EcoLodge:
https://www.kapawi.com

Fundación Pachamama:
https://www.pachamama.org.ec/en/

The Work That Reconnects:
https://workthatreconnects.org

Earth Guardians:
https://www.earthguardians.org

Fridays for Future:
https://fridaysforfuture.org

Rainforest Alliance:
https://www.rainforest-alliance.org

Rainforest Trust:
https://www.rainforesttrust.org

Jane Goodall Institute:
https://janegoodall.org

Panthera: https://panthera.org

World Wildlife Fund:
https://www.worldwildlife.org

Wildlife Conservation Society:
https://www.wcs.org

Center for Biological Diversity:
https://www.biologicaldiversity.org

Survival International:
https://www.survivalinternational.org

Climate Psychology Alliance:
https://www.climatepsychologyalliance.org

Palmless, working to end rainforest destruction
https://www.gopalmless.com

Acknowledgements

I am grateful to the Achuar People for sharing their remarkable dream culture and reaching out to the "people of the Global North" in their tireless efforts to protect the rainforest and change the dream of the modern world.

The Pachamama Alliance and its founders, John Perkins, Bill and Lynne Twist, for responding to their outreach with passion, integrity, and dedication. Your efforts provided inspiration for this story.

Kapawi Ecolodge, for your mission of establishing and maintaining not only an exemplary ecolodge but also an informative and beautiful website. Your efforts enabled me to learn about and share your vision with others.

Christina Serrano Jacobs, your thoughtful, informed, and critical review of the story helped me portray the Achuar culture of the Ecuadorian Amazon as factually as possible. Thank you.

Publisher, Karen Kilpatrick, and the team at Genius Cat Books, for your ongoing support and encouragement.

Editor, Alexis Latshaw, for your keen eye, warm heart, enthusiasm for storytelling, and patience.

Illustrator, book designer, and creative collaborator, Melisca Klisanin, for your artistry, inspiration, and dedication to this project.

Beth Brett, for your encouragement and invaluable support in helping spread the word about the Chronicles of G.A.I.A. series.

Starr Library in Rhinebeck, NY for providing a friendly and supportive environment for artists and writers.

My family and friends, for showing up in the most loving, thoughtful, supportive, and celebratory ways. I love you, each and all.

Scholars, authors, and teachers whose works inform this book and to whom I am deeply grateful: John Perkins, Joanna Macy, Ervin László; Jeremy Narby, Ruth Inge-Heinze, Stanley Krippner, Simon Buxton, and Martín Prechtel.

Jaguar, for reminding us to touch our fears. *May you flourish.*